Horse Play

Matters of the Heart
By

Melissa M Marlow

HORSE PLAY: Matters of the Heart

Copyright © 2016 by Melissa M Marlow

Print ISBN: ISBN-10:0-9835245-8-0
                     ISBN-13:978-0-9835245-8-8

Cover Design and Interior format by Poehler Publishing

1 *Reveal*

The thud of someone knocking at my door led me to wonder who would be up at this hour. I walked out of my bedroom and the perfect image of a young woman silhouetted in the window of the door. Irritated Tracy would be trying to tempt me again. Determined to take her over my knee and whip her butt for coming on to me. I took a deep breath to control myself I opened the door full of determination, "I told you no! You need to stop..."

Shock stopped my scolding when I noticed it wasn't Tracy. My heart jumped at the sight of Samantha standing there. She radiated a glow reminding me she is the perfect little angle.

Her eyes wide with wonder and her mouth opened with an unsaid question. She entered when I opened the door for her. Normally she came for my stories, but this time her visit is unexpected.

Thick with regret for yelling I tried to recover, "Sorry, I thought you were someone else."

Dragging her feet, her head down, and the sullen facial expression; told me it's going to be a serious visit.

In her attempts to be herself she replied, "I didn't know you had many visitors."

Waiting with wonder, my eyes followed her over to the bookshelf. A grin took over my face. She is here for a story. Waiting for her to pick the picture of her choice my mind raced with ideas to make her laugh.

In the past she would search out the pictures to find one that spiked her interest. Today her hand moved slowly to each picture not choosing one, her shoulders raised and lowered in a way that shows she is struggling with something, and the small sniffle told me something is wrong, "Sam?"

Allowing her time to collect her thoughts I detected her trembling hand trace over a couple more pictures. She procrastinated at telling me what is bothering her.

Maybe she needed a little help, so I asked, "You didn't come here for the stories, Samantha. What is wrong?"

When she turned to me the glisten of one tear ran down her cheek. She took a deep breath and released what she needed to say, "I'm late."

My insides twisted, my lungs collapsed, and my heart stopped as if I died. Deep down in my gut I knew this punishment is for every impure idea I had of making love to her. It went against everything I believed. I did love her and hoped someday, when she's a lot older, we'd get married. I didn't want to say the wrong thing, but the words escaped from my mouth before grasping what she had just said, "Whose?"

Obviously, this killed me. In her wide eyes, as blue as the Caribbean Sea, the tears gathered hinting at over flowing. We stared for minutes, which seemed like hours. Without her reply I knew whose child it would be... My nephew's name came from my mouth again without hesitation, "Jarod!"

Her plump bottom lip trembled as the tears spilled over and ran down those smooth rosy cheeks.

This is my punishment for loving a child in the ways of my dreams? Blackness caved in around me and my voice cracked as I asked another question involuntarily, "Why?"

Not wanting to ever let her go again, I stared into those eyes. The crease in her forehead, the sad eyes, and the pouty lips gave her regrets away. I hoped she saw the pain she caused me. Waiting for her to say something my body intensified filling with something even I had a hard time subduing.

She blubbered out, "You kiss Tracy."

I guessed her answer reflected the way I looked to her because her eyes avoided me now.

My heart pounded so hard while my pulse echoed in my ears; an excruciating jabbed to my temples made me close my eyes in agony. My hands fisted with the question in my head. Is this revenge? I didn't deserve revenge. Punishment for being in love with her, for my fantasies of things we do? Yes! But not revenge. It's obvious I'm not the least bit interested in her sister. I never spent any time with her, talked to her, or anything with her sister. Why she'd think I'd kiss her sister, especially sense I am in love with..? My jaw clinched as I tried to keep calm, "What you think you saw... Tracy kissed me... What you didn't see... What I did do, was push her away. I sent her back to the house!"

A sobbing gasp escaped her, and a full stream of tears flowed from her eyes. She tried to wipe them swiftly, but too many to hold them back.

Not being able to separate my anger from the longing to hold her ripped my heart to pieces. All I wanted to do is wrap my arms around her and take away all the sadness. I wanted to tell her everything would be okay. I am in love with her and I would take care of *IT* and *her* if she'd let me. The only problem with this theory is I wouldn't allow myself to have her, and what if she loved..., "Do you love him?"

Her eyes flashed blue as they bore into mine while shaking her head. My knees went weak with relief. In a whisper, between sobs, came out three words that defused my anger, "He's like you."

I held motionless wondering what she tried to say. Did she tell me she had sex with Jarod because she wants to make love to me? No, that is not a good reason to do that with him. Does that mean she tried to get my attention, and this just happened? Now she will never experience how I truly love her because I won't act on my desires, but I will protect her.

Time is what I needed to evaluate the situation. Needing to sort through what she said, what happened, and what I'm going to do to protect her, "I need a day to think about this."

That came out colder than I meant. Hurt and devastation is what I saw on her face with my reply. Pulling her into my arms right now would be very dangerous because I'd slip and tell her everything. The confession would be that I've always wanted her, that I've always loved her, and that I want to be the one to take care of her the rest of her life. The sad part is she's too young and confused to understand this now. Samantha moved quickly to the door, stopped and wiped her tears, and hesitated long enough to say one last thing, "If I am... I don't want it."

She didn't move. Was she waiting for me to say something to make it all go away? I knew it would be wrong to get rid of the fetus, but I didn't want her to want it. Wanting to take the pressure from her I said, "Give me a day or two. I will figure something out."

Samantha stayed still waiting for me to do something, so I took a step closer. It's time to tell her that every touch we shared burned into my soul. I took another step towards her. Needing to tell her she meant everything to me and I would help her through this no matter what happens. Reaching out to take her into my arms, but my hands didn't reach her in time.

She blurted out, "I Don't Want IT!" She raced off at full speed.

Falling to my hands and knees wasn't how I wanted to react to this, but it happened anyway. A wave of emotions came over my body and pulled me in deeper and deeper until I could no longer breathe. I hadn't experienced hyperventilation since my father passed away. Between losing Samantha and killing my own flesh and blood; it was too much for me.

No matter what, talking to Jarod now is not a choice. I might beat him. Forcing myself back to bed I laid down staring at the ceiling until tears trickled out the sides. As I closed them my mind drifted to Samantha on the first day I met this annoying precious child full of questions.

2 The Arrival

The day I arrived at the William's Ranch for my interview with Kyle Williams he introduced me to this horrible, wonderful, adorable, pain in my ass of a child. Love at first sight did happen with Samantha. She's a girl that grows on you.

Mr. Williams lead me around his small ranch while he explained what he needed from me if I took the job. Being a trainer is what I thought I would become, but his offer would make me one now. Along with taking care of the horse's daily needs. They wanted someone good, but couldn't afford a big name trainer so they were willing to give me a shot.

The offer seemed okay, but at 19 years of age I didn't need much. I'd have a place of my own, a little shack on the property. It had two small bedrooms big enough for a double bed, a night stand, and a dresser in each. The Kitchen is an ell shape with a sink, stove, fridge, and very little counter space. There is only room enough for a small table and two chairs. The living room isn't much bigger with only enough room for a love seat, a small TV stand, and two book shelves off to the sides. Of course the meals would be included, plus $200 a week. For me this would be my new home with Mr. Williams's willingness to take a chance on me.

Next we made our way out and about the ranch. First the stables, then grooming area, Mr. Williams's office, and last my office. At 19 I am going to have an office. After that we moved down the lane where he showed me all the pastures. The more I saw the happier I became to make this my new home and my new future.

We got back to the riding rink, and he asked me what I thought about everything. A little shocked that he hadn't asked me any questions I'm a little skeptical to reply in a positive way. He continued to explain how he wanted the ranch to run when I noticed a little girl walking towards us. That's when I first met Samantha, who would turn out to be the love of my life, even though I didn't know it at the time.

Before he got distract with his family I had to ask, "Mr. Williams, don't you have any questions for me?"

He laughed, but I didn't get why he would laugh at me, but he pointed to the little girl, "I don't, but she will. And the job is yours if she chooses you."

Stunned that he could leave this decision up to a child my eyes bulged with disbelief. Kyle hugged Samantha, "I like him so if he passes your tests he stays."

She didn't introduce herself. Her eyes looked me up and down before she took my hand. She pulled me toward the stables as I glanced back over my shoulder at Mr. Williams wondering if he was serious. A child shouldn't be deciding my fate; she's not even my age. She wouldn't be able to tell if I am capable of doing the job or not. What my qualifications are? What's involved in training, or anything that has to do with horses? Why would he leave it up to her?

I definitely have the job if she's deciding because I will just use a little playful charm and she'll be an easy push over. Her questions seemed easy enough in the beginning. My name, where I grew up, and how many years did I work with horses, and what I liked most about the job. Amused with her I still wondered why she'd get to decide my fate.

We got to the first stall. She turned to me with her eyebrows raise, "Now is the real test. This is Blaze. He has something wrong with him. I want you to tell me what you find." She opened the stall, so I walked in not wanting to take my eyes off of her. *So, this is how it's going to go with her?*

She nodded her head for me to take a look at him.

Not trusting her knowledge I traced my hand over every inch of his body. I checked his teeth, hoofs, and checked out all the muscles on his legs looking for any swelling. He had none. I stopped and peaked at her wondering if she's just testing me on something not there. This is a test so it could be a trick question. She grinned from ear to ear, and she giggled a little when I glared at her. If there's anything wrong with him I will find it. I moved in front of the horse running my hands along his neck, down the crest, and checked his teeth. Pinching his skin I huffed with satisfaction of finding something. I walked over to her, glared at her while trying to hold back my satisfied grin, and shook my head with disapproval.

She spoke with a know it all voice, "Well, what do you think is wrong with him?"

"Other than needing a bath, he's a little dehydrated."

"He is not!"

Proud of myself I assured her, "Yes, he is."

Her lips pierced, her eyes grew angry, "NOT! I take good care of him."

This time I took her hand in mine and led her to the front of the horse. Keeping her hand in mine I showed her how to check him for dehydration, "When you pinch here, see how the skin doesn't pop back out?"

Her eyes met mine with determination, "Yes, and he is not dehydrated."

"Well, I hate to tell you this, but you're wrong."

She walked out and grabbed a hose, refilled his stock tank, and huffed at me. I chuckled while I waited for her to finish filling the tank.

She took me by the hand again and we walked to the next stall, giving me the mare's name Star. Again holding out her hand for me to go in and check her. I did the same evaluation. She had splints, but I didn't stop when I found that problem. Continuing with the evaluation I went over everything before peaking over Star at her, "What's your name?"

She raised her eyebrows at me and didn't reply. Not sure if I want the job if I need to prove myself to her, but everything else is so perfect that I could handle her.

Avoiding my question she asks, "Well, do you have any idea yet?"

Standing back up to glare at her, "Yes, she has splints."

"What? No way! I take care of my horses." She walked over and stood in front of me waiting for me to show her without asking me to show her. I took her hand and traced down Star's front leg until we felt the swelling together. She pulled her hand away, turned to me, looked me up and down again, and a crooked little smirk appeared on that little face. She handed me the reins without a word. As soon as I had the reins on Star this child took my hand again and led me out the gate, "Bring Star."

I followed, and she brought me to another room where they care for the horses.

Not showing me where anything was she stopped her foot and demanded, "Show me how to help her."

Searching every draw and every cabinet while she made her way to the counter top I pulled out the things needed. I would glance over at her catching her watching me out of the corner of her eye, but she didn't want me to see her scrutiny. Instead she laughed and giggled, finding enjoyment in my struggles to find things.

When everything was ready I spoke to her while doing each step. The funniest thing; she already knew how to do this.

My whole day filled with different tasks while she evaluated everything I did.

At 6 pm we headed to the main house, but she wasn't giving me any clue of what she's going to decide. She pulled me to the sink in the mud room to wash up for dinner. As we both scrubbed I had to ask, "So, how did I do?"

She laughed at me handing me a towel. I wiped my hands leisurely hoping she would answer me. As soon as I set the towel down she had my hand in hers and she led me to a large dining table. Mr. Williams, Mrs. Williams, and another girl are all seated and waiting for us. She shoved me into an empty chair and then she sat next to me. The other girl looked and seemed older than this child. Maybe she was the one I needed on my side because this child didn't seem to care for me. Before anyone spoke they all folded their hands, the child folded mine for me, and then pushed my head down for the prayer. They said there thanks together for the food we were about to eat. At home we didn't pray regularly, but they kept it simple enough. My head down I kept an eye on the child from the corner of my eye. She's quit the specimen.

She piled food on my plate for me a lot more than I would have taken myself. I put my hand up to stop her from putting more on my plate not wanting them to think I would eat them out of house and home. I sat and ate silently as they all talked easily about different things.

When Mr. Williams finished eating he leaned back in his chair with his hands behind his head, "Well, Sam, how did he do?"

She shrugged her shoulders acting like she didn't think I was that great, "He seems to know a few things."

Mr. Williams spoke again, "So, do we keep him?"

She took her time Hum-ing and Ha-ing. Waiting for my fate, my eyes went back and forth between them. She reviewed a few things to her dad that I'm surprised she noticed. That's a good sign. She stood up sharply but hesitated for the longest minute that I have ever experienced. It got harder and harder to sit there without saying anything on my behalf.

She finally spoke, "He stays."

Relief exploded in my chest. I stood to shake Mr. Williams's hand, but as swiftly as I took his hand in mine for a hand shake she pulled me away.

Mr. Williams spoke out quickly, "You should call me Kyle."

But his voice faded as I went out the room, then out of the house following her.

She walked into the shack as if she owned it. She gave a brief rundown of where things were and then laid out bedding for me.

Her direction came out strong, "You have a TV, but I wouldn't stay up to late though. I will be back at 5am. We start work early around here. There is an alarm clock in your room. Do you need my help to set it?"

Her eyes met mine, and for the first time she radiated innocence. The color of blue in her eyes had their very own stunning shade.

Gawking at her made her confrontational, but her eyes stunned me into a state of blatant staring. I grinned and replied, "No, I can do it by myself." I didn't want her to know that I get up a little earlier than that.

Hesitating she said, "Okay."

Looking around the shack one more time to see if there was anything else she could tell me, but she only huffed and then said, "How old are you?"

Not knowing if the interrogations were going to continue I replied, "Nineteen, but I grew..."

Putting up her hand she stopped me, "Well, that's all."

I caught her name at the dinner table so I addressed her, "Hey Sam?"

She turned glaring at me, "Its Samantha for you. We feed horses first in the morning then we eat. After breakfast I will show you the grounds. Make sure you are up on time. I don't like to wait."

I had every intention of getting on her good side, "Samantha, how old are you?"

She gave me a firm look, but cracked a smile, "Well, I'm not the one on probation."

That surprised me, "Probation?"

"Yes, I will give you a chance to prove yourself for three months. I want someone who can follow a schedule and who knows what they are doing. So be ready for more questions tomorrow."

The smile on her face as she turned around and walked out told me I could win her approval with time. I moved to the door to watch her run to the house with her dirty brown hair flying behind her. Kyle waited for her, standing at the top of the steps. They talked shortly, they hugged, and then he swatted her rear to push her inside the house. It put a smile on my face to see a loving family. Kyle attention came to me. He tipped his hat to me, turned to the house, and followed in after her.

I went to my room setting the alarm for 4 am. I always started earlier than 5 am, plus I had plans of taking a tour of the stables alone before I had to deal with the over bearing child again.

3 Unspoken

I drifted back to the present time. My smile tarnished by what she had told me. How would I ever guess five years ago that today I would be in love with her?

Morning would come quickly, so I needed to sleep, but worrying about Samantha kept me restless. The pleasant things about her are what I should concentrate on. Her crystal blue eyes penetrating my soul, her smile brightening my worst days, and her demeanor I wanted to stifle with my kisses. Back to kissing her was not a good thing.

Starting over with how unruly her sandy brown hair usually is, except when she has it in a ponytail, or curled under her cowboy hat. This isn't going to work if I found good within the bad. I told myself to try again.

How about those old flannel shirts of her dads she wore when she worked with me. They did nothing for her figure until she got tired of pulling it up and she would tie it at the waist. Oh her waist that sometimes peaked out when reaching up to get on a horse. This is ridiculous. Can't I find anything about her that repulses me at all anymore? Her legs, that's it. Contoured in muscles, long, and looked particularly thin when she wore cut off jean shorts. How strong they would be wrapped around me? Shit!

I rolled over in my bed covering my face with my arm. How will I ever sleep again when all I can see is everything I love about this girl? There had to be a bad side... She had slept with another man, but he happened to be my nephew. She might be pregnant. She's stubborn, out spoken, opinionated, and worst of it impatient, though I wanted her to be mine, someday. Why couldn't she just wait a little longer so we could have a future together? I had every intension of telling her how I felt when she was older. Like 20 maybe. Now is not the right time, never would be the right time. I had to get her and this idea, out of my head.

Unless...

Unless I said the baby is mine. If it were mine she would have to marry me, her parents wouldn't be happy about it, but I am like family already. If Kyle didn't kill me first, he would eventually come around to seeing that it would be for the best. And the best part would be that she would be mine. Of course I would be forcing her to be with me and I would have to be a father to my nephew's child.

No matter how I look at it, we would have to figure something else out, she said she didn't want it.

STOP!!! I rolled over pulling the pillow over my head. Think blackness, think blackness, think blackness. Finally it came.

4 The Game

My dreams brought me back to the second day. How I got up early going out to check the horses over before she showed up and asked me questions. Her reaction of storming into the barn yelling for me made me chuckle.

"Kamron! Kamron! Are you out here?"

Panic in her voice rather than that demanding bossy tone she had the day previous. Her feet hit the ground hard and fast with her search. She wanted me here, and she didn't even realize it yet. I came out leaning against the stall of the first horse she showed me, Blaze.

Coming to a halt the instant her eyes found me. They filled with a blazing anger, "I thought you gave up already. Maybe it's too hard for you."

"Nope. *I* get up around 4 am to begin my work day. *You* didn't give me a chance to tell you."

She scowled at me as she went from stall to stall making sure all the horses are cared for and fed. We spent the whole morning together with little scrutiny from her. I found it amusing that she wasn't full of attitude today. I allowed her to lead me to the house about 9:00 am for breakfast. She seemed to treat me like one of her ponies leading me everywhere. We washed up together, and I gave her a shove, "So, how did I do this morning?"

The roll of her eyes left me feeling less than what she expected. With a scowl she put me in my place, "It's the first day. We'll see."

After breakfast we headed back out. Next, she wanted to test my abilities of grooming. We walked into the cool down room and she handed me the brush and comb.

Expectant she said matter of fact, "It's all included. Understanding how to do everything is needed to be a good trainer, right?"

Shaking my head and laughing I moved to groom the horse. She took a seat on the counter to watch.

The oddest thing happened; Blaze fidgeted as if being spooked when I brushed down to his stomach. When he shifted I stopped to stroke him with a calming voice, "it's okay boy."

Trying it again he shifted, stomped, and neighed. I wiped my hand over his underside in search of finding what bothers him, but he had already calmed.

Samantha seemed to enjoy that the horse didn't like me brushing him, or checking his belly.

Something wasn't right, and I smelled a rat. I started again, but as I moved the brush down to Blaze's stomach I glanced over his back. Clicking noise came from her, and that is when Blaze shifted tensely. She's irritating him on purpose. Steaming with irritation I walked around Blaze to stand in front of her, waiting for an explanation. Trying to keep her innocence she barked, "What?"

I didn't have time for games, particularly her games. I pulled her down, tucked her under my arm intending to kick her out while I worked on Blaze, and headed for the door. She kicked and screamed the whole way, and I didn't have to struggle to hold her off until I closed the door and lock it. It shuttered with every punch and kick she threw at it, and the profanity that came from her mouth floored me. I laughed and went back to work. Blaze cooperated with ease in his calmer state after I removed the problem.

Not long after it got quiet I finished. Taking my time I walked Blaze to his stall. Greeted not by Samantha alone, but she had her father with her. Fire danced in her eyes as I moved closer to them.

Kyle was first to speak, "So, may I ask why you treated my daughter this way?"

I glared at Samantha, because she knew dam well why I treated her that way, but I spoke to Kyle, "Samantha deliberately irritated Blaze while I groomed him."

Samantha didn't wait for her father to respond she bellowed out, "Did not! *You* weren't doing it right. Don't blame..."

I would not let her do this, "SAMANTHA! Do you want to play these games?" I shook my head glaring at her, "I know what I am doing!"

Her eyes went large with shock. The conflict in her brain twisting its way until a twitch of a grin grew on her mouth, "Yeah. I picked on Blaze. But, I was testing you!"

Our gazes locked on, each other as if to challenge one another.

I think he surprised us both when Kyle chuckled. That is when our bond broke. He patted me on the back, "I have seen no one take that approach with her. Good for you."

"DAD!"

He turned to walk away but gave his input, "Samantha, behave!"

Wanting to avoid gloating I avoided looking at her and waited. She must have been avoiding me also because we stood there for far too long. Knowing it wouldn't be good to look at her I glanced over to her. Our timing was right on because she sneaked a peek at me too. The connection way too long, and too much of a power struggle between us, I had to say something, "What's next?"

If steam could have come out her ears it would have. She stormed onward as I followed. Keeping a foot or two between us we moved on to the next item on her list. At least she wouldn't be playing any games soon with being leery of me.

We headed down the lane. Watching Samantha's vise grip on the rains; no wonder Blaze acted so temperamental with every little thing she did. How could her dad have so much faith in her when she still seemed to struggle on so many things with taking care of the horses. I had to say something, but it would not go well with her, "You tell me you take good care of your horses, but you're forcing him." Moving closer and reaching for her hands, "He knows you. Don't use force." I loosened her fingers, "Like this. The slightest movement from you he will understand, and he won't defy your guidance."

Pleased that she allowed me to show her something, I grinned, "He wants to please you."

I held back a little to watch her with the knowledge of something better. Testing how much control she had; she moved him this way, that way, and then turned back. Her expression didn't give away anything. Not knowing if she's happy with the results or irritated about me being right I asked, "Better?"

She held back a grin, "Yeah, I guess."

Roaming the grounds she reviewed what her father showed me, but we were going further than that. The lane leads to a creek, which we followed down to another lane, and then back out to the main road. From my calculations we were about a mile and half from the ranch. Samantha pointed to houses along the way giving me the names of the owners, and their family backgrounds. She has intimate details about each of them and had no problem sharing the info with me.

After spending the day with her it clear she will be a handful, no matter how well I did my job. So much for having a life outside of work, with her hanging out down here.

5 Nightmare

I woke covered in sweat, my blanket and sheet entangled my legs. Everything that ran through my head over the last few days, terrorized me in my sleep.

Worry, sadness, betrayal, and being messed up clued me into the truest feelings I had for Samantha. Not being able to tell her all these years is wrong even though I did it to protect her no matter how miserable it made me.

Now what am I going to do? That's the question that kept running through my head but the answer did not.

If she chose someone else I couldn't tell her how I felt. If she is pregnant, it's someone else's. That someone happens to be my nephew. No matter how I looked at this I knew my feelings didn't matter anymore. I needed to put them away and let her go.

Over the last five years, in the back of my mind, for reasons unknown to me I assumed we would eventually be together. My plan to wait for her to finish college might have been a little too long of a wait. But I wanted to give her a chance to get a job, have a career, and then we'd spend quality time together, and let the friendship develop into… yes, a loving relationship. The age difference has always been an issue for me, but if we waited until she's 24 it wouldn't really matter anymore. The age difference is part of it, and now thinking she is pregnant, well it broke my heart.

I lay back with my arm over my eyes. I required sleep. If only this nightmare would go away.

6 Competition

Samantha at 12 years old, had her first riding competition. We spent months perfecting her technique, her posture, her control, and the routine in which she would ride. Blaze took to it all because he wanted to please Samantha. When Samantha complained I pushed her harder, and when that didn't work I joined her on Blaze.

Distraction is what I experienced. The sweet magnolia scent mixed with green apples drifted to my sense of smell and made my mouth water.

Ignoring the sensation I held her hands in mine. We gripped the reins together with my arms wrapped around her. I pressed my leg in and adjusted the reins to teach Blaze what I wanted him to do, and to show her that it's not all in the reins. Day after day I held my arms around her to teach her the best ways to work with Blaze so he performs the way we needed him too.

It seemed like little time had passed when it came time for the show. Standing there in the waiting station I went over everything again one step at a time. With observing her go through it in her head, allowed me to be more self-assured. Her father, Kyle didn't make me nervous, but Samantha wanted to be perfect for him.

They called her name. Her eyes shot to mine. Instead of being filled with confidence they swelled with worry. Her mouth twitch when she claimed, "I can't do this."

I needed to be supportive, "You are here. You've practiced for months. You have a natural instinct. Blaze distinguishes what you tell him. Guide him, don't command. Trust me."

I lifted her up to his back. Uncertainty filled her face as she surveyed me while I double checked everything. The way her eyes bore into me made me want to give her more, but there wasn't anything else. My chest hurt because of it. Taking one last glimpse at her face the eyes pleaded.

I had to reassure her. I patted her leg, "Samantha, it's your first competition and you have nothing to lose. You are absolutely ready."

With this she nodded, straightened herself in the saddle, took a deep breath, and headed off. I went to stand at the gate to keep my eyes on her. Confident in her ability I didn't worried about how she would do. My main concern seemed to be her getting hurt somehow.

Kyle came and stood next to me, "You did well with her."

Holding my breath I gasped to reply, "Not yet. Let's wait to see how she does."

He laughed at me. How could he laugh at a time like this?

He elaborated, "I mean she is nicer. She looks up to you, and that doesn't happen for her."

I glanced over for a moment. There had to be someone

He pointed to the ring. Samantha had started her routine, but he spoke as we observed, "It's hard to look up to someone when you know more than most. You have showed her things she didn't know."

My attention went back to her. I don't think he could sense I too am attached to her.

With every challenging move I held my breath. With turns I gasped. When she completed her run and headed our way I let go of my nervousness and resumed breathing. She did an amazing job, but we had to wait to see what the judges decided.

We all sat around and waited except for Samantha. I took Blaze off to cool him down while she paced back and forth. I wanted to grab her and hug her, but that is her family's job to do. She paced her way over to Blaze and me, but she wanted to talk to him. She praised him over and over, but it my hunch that she is reassuring herself that they did good.

I took a carrot from my pocket and moved close to her. I took her hand in mine. When she realized what I gave her a huge grin grew on her face.

Her eyes pierced into mine as her eyebrows rose, "You're not supposed to do that."

Justifying myself I claimed, "It's a special treat, and it's good for him."

She rolled her eyes, but moved to feed it to him.

Moving closer to her again I held out an award that had been mine when I use to ride.

Those blue eyes came up to stare at me with wonder, "I can't take this. You earned this."

I grinned and proclaimed, "And so have you."

"Why don't you both turn so we can get a picture of the two of you?"

Startled by her mother's words I stepped away from her. She didn't let me get far before she grabbed my waist and hugged me there. I put my hand on her shoulder as they took the picture of us together. I hid my admiration for Samantha behind my grin.

At the awards we lined up. The riders, the horses, and trainers all moved to the front line. I stood behind Samantha not wanting the attention, but when they called her name for third place I jumped in place and yelled, "YEAH!" so much for not wanting attention. She walked up and got her award. After the first place ribbon got awarded I picked Samantha up in a huge hug congratulating her. She didn't even hug me back. She wasn't happy, but ecstatic seemed like a mild statement of how much pride and joy that ran through me now.

After all the pictures and congratulation's we headed home. With her mopping all the way home I tried to tease, poke, and prod her into play, but she wouldn't have anything to do with it. I knew the next competition would be a personal challenge for her because she's not going to settle for anything less than first place.

Horse Play

7 Negative

I woke finding myself looking at the ceiling again. I rolled from the bed and went out to the living room picking up the picture from her first competition. The gleam in her eyes, the smile on her face, and when she wrapped her arms around me for a photo, that's when I started to have feelings for her. Not like creepy or anything. I needed to make her happy, to take care of her, to be there for her for everything she needed help with. Apparently she is a child, being 12 years old, but I am falling in love with her. How can I deny these emotions, and how am I going to deny my desires now?

God how I wanted to take her in my arms, hold her tight, and tell her everything will be all right, because I loved her and would take care of her. But I wouldn't do *that*.

I started my day early and went through my regular routine. Jared tagged along but determined to work him harder I ordered him to do more.

Watching him put his heart into the task at hand made me ponder about her and him together. Did he take advantage of Samantha, push her into it? Or was it her? My temperature was running hot having him there with me. I wanted to smack him upside the head and ask him what the hell did he do, but that wouldn't solve the problem. The issue being that Samantha may be pregnant and what we would do about it.

My head seemed to go wild with ideas of what I would do if she came down and he is here. Would I stop him from talking to her, or would it be better to let them work it out?

Why do teenagers have to be so stupid?

Horse Play

When we finished our morning chores and Samantha hadn't appeared, I assumed it would be best if we didn't go up to the house for breakfast. Instead we went to the shack. Jared asked no questions. He got a pan out and the eggs, he set out salt and pepper, and put bread in the toaster while I whipped up scrambled eggs. We ate in silence. He must have known I am upset because as soon as he finished eating he got up and ran the water for dishes. He washed up his own and the pan. I heard the shower after he left the kitchen. What is that boy up too? Not taking long he came back out in jeans, a white beater top, and his work boots on. He saw me look him up and down. His breath came out in a chuckle, "What's next?"

He looked like a teenage model so there was no way he is getting close to Samantha, "Back fence."

It didn't take us long to load up what we needed and headed to the back of the property. Anger is not a healthy emotion, but what he did to my innocent Samantha is beyond forgiveness keeping me angry with him.

"Is something wrong?"

Like he didn't have a clue what is wrong. My only reply came in one word, "Yep."

Silence would be better than him talking, but teenagers can't keep their mouths shut. "Do you want to talk about it?"

"Hah! No I don't!"

Jared's eyes penetrated me. Aware that I am upset with him he didn't get it that all my anger is directed at him. When I pulled up to the spot we were working today he turned eager to find out why I'm so angry.

"Is it Samantha? I haven't seen her in a few days and if something is wrong I might be able to help her. I see her talking to you, and I just think if I talked..."

"You just thought?"

"Yes, I want to help too. I like her."

Blood rush through my body at an elevated pace. I turned my glare to him, "YOU LIKE HER?"

He nodded and seemed generally concerned about her. He almost looked innocent, but not quiet.

Blood boiling beyond reason I didn't elaborate, got out of the truck, and unloaded the supplies. I had to get rid of this anger or I just may kill him out here and hide the body. He didn't push the issue and helped to get the load out. I got him started and went back to get more supplies. I had to put distance between us to clear my head.

Working to load the truck by myself Samantha came down from the house. I kept loading, and she followed me back and forth. This is the saddest I have ever seen her. She watched the ground when she walked, but she dragged her feet. In fact her whole body drooped with sadness. How am I going to cheer her up with all her worries hanging over her head? This isn't what I planned, that's for sure. I glanced over to her wondering if she had something to say, but nothing came from her mouth. No gleam in her eyes, no brightness to her face. Not wanting to see her like this I still didn't stop glancing at her every chance I might.

When the truck was filled with the load she leaned against it next to the driver's door. Good lord I am in trouble here. My thoughts wanted to sweep her off her feet and hold her so tight. If I made this better by wrapping my arms around her and embrace her with love I would do that now. I wanted to whisper in her ear, *I love you Samantha and I will take care of you*, but that isn't happening. Staying silent I waited for her to speak.

Her words spilled from her mouth, "Did you come up with anything?"

I shook my head, "Need a few days."

She nodded and walked back towards the house. It killed me to not give her a solution I could share with her yet.

Keeping Jared and Samantha apart also made it so I didn't get to see her either. After four days she appeared. Except it's not what I expected to hear from her, "I have to tell him."

I have failed her, "No, I said I would take care of it."

"So what am I supposed to do while you try to come up with something?"

"Give me a few more days to...."

Her voice on the brink of tears she stopped me, "But it's already been a few days and you aren't doing anything."

I had to do something drastic, so at least it looked like I had been working on figuring out how to help her, "I am sending Jared home tomorrow."

Now her eyes filled with tears, "What? What about..., you know?" Her eyes darted to her belly, and it shredded my heart.

With more determination I repeated, "I will take care of it."

She swallowed her dismay, "But it's his responsibility."

What is she saying, "Do you want him to stay?"

She's confused but if she loved him than she needed to tell me now.

She shook her head no, but replied, "I'm not sure what I want."

What did she mean she's not sure, "Do you love him?"

With a raised voice she scolded, "No. I told you that."

Now she's making me angry, "Why did you do it with him then?"

I guess I asked the wrong question. She stormed away from me crying. I hurt her and all I wanted to do is love her, to kiss those plumb lips, and wipe those tears away. I felt horrible for hurting her because when you love someone you don't hurt them this way. But she hurt me with what she did with my nephew. She had to sense my feelings so why did she do it? I should have told her all along. This mess is so confusing and I shouldn't have desires for her, but I did. It's wrong in so many ways it's difficult for me to sort them out.

I brought Jared to the bus station the next day. He didn't understand why I'm sending him home so soon. He kept asking questions the whole way, but I bit my tongue to keep from slicing him to shreds with it. We got to the bus station, and I stopped the truck, but I had to express why I'm so angry, "Did you have sex with Samantha?"

He stared at me blankly with his mouth hanging open empty of a reply.

He wasn't even grown up enough to answer me with an honest reply. Anger seeped into every aching muscle. I forced myself to move away from him, with his innocent stare. I grabbed his bag, walked over to the passenger side of the truck, and pulled him from it. He stood there dumfounded stunned by my question. I shook my head trying to understand why he acted so innocent.

His eyes wide with shock, "Did she tell you that?"

Does he think I am stupid, that I don't understand what it's like to be a teenager, "Yes, and now you have to leave."

He pleaded with me, "But, it wasn't like that. This isn't my fault. Damn, I really liked her."

There's that word again, *like*.

Fiery filled every inch of my body, while I put my hand to his chest pinning him to the truck, "If you liked her you shouldn't have done that. If she is pregnant it would put an end to her dreams."

He didn't seem worried that I wanted to kill him at this exact moment. He gasped, "What? She's pregnant?"

I closed my eyes not wanting to see his concern for her. No one loves her the way I do, and it hurt to see something in his eyes. His worry about her tore me up. I glared into his eyes, "She's late and you need to leave now."

He shook his head disagreeing with me, "No. I can take care of this. I need to talk to her. Look, I will marry her."

That just about through me over the edge, "Now wouldn't that be a great idea?"

He grabbed my shirt pushing his way back to the truck, "I need to stay. I need to talk to her. We need to figure this out because it wasn't like that."

Yeah, he didn't love her that's why it isn't like that. Floored that he wanted to go back and talk to her. I pinned him again boring my eyes deep into his, "I have this handled. This mess will get clean up by me, and you need to go home because right now all I want to do is kill you."

Making my point it registered that the anger I held restrained, could kill him. He got on the bus not happy, but he did what I wanted him to do, go home.

After picking up a pregnancy test and driving back to the ranch I had a lot more time to consider this. Samantha wanted a solution, and she wanted me to come up with it. Jared had the right idea when it came down to *it*. I would offer to marry her if she wanted to keep the baby. That way I wasn't taking care of the problem I would also take care of her.

When I got back to the ranch I found her sitting on a bale of hay outside of the stables. I made my way to her, but saw she had her arms wrapped around her waist, and a strained face.

Our eyes met. Her eyes filled with questions though she asked one, "You sent him home?'"

"Yeah, if you don't love him it would be best if I sent him away."

Agreeing with a nod she had the hint of appreciation cross her face. Looking around to make sure we were alone I pulled out the small paper bag, "Samantha, I have an idea." I handed her the bag, "We should find out first before we figure out what to do. It's a pregnancy test."

She looked around carefully before she pulled the box from the bag. As she examined the directions her eyes filled with tears. I didn't want to upset her more, but we needed to find out for sure.

With encouragement I add, "Go get it over with. I'll wait right her for you and we can see what it says together."

Her eyes flashed to mine again. With her eyebrows raised, and the pursed lips, a doubtful expression filled her face. I walked with her to the restroom in the barn and she glanced at me as she closed the door. I couldn't conceive what she felt right now.

The test was simple. Pull it out, pee on the stick, and then wait. So why is it taking her so long to come back out?

She came out holding the stick in her hand like its dirty or disgusting.

"So what does it say?"

Shrugging her shoulders, "It's supposed to take five minutes."

Now we wait. Samantha paced back and forth in front of me making me nervous just watching her.

Kyle walked in, "So, are we taking a break or what is going on down here?"

Sam turned to her dad moving her hand with the pregnancy stick behind her back, "No, we're..." loss of word panic filled her face as she glanced at me for the answer.

"No, I'm trying to talk her into entering another competition."

"Well, that's a fine idea. Are you hinting at one in particular?"

"Yes, the Grade Marie Tartain's is coming up."

He clapped his hand, "The Tartain's is a great competition. We would get a lot of exposure."

Kyle wrapped Samantha into his side while I grabbed the stick from her hand. They continued all the way out of the barn walking towards the house. Not following, my mind set on the test stick that would tell us if she is pregnant. Locking myself in the bathroom I pulled it out of my pocket. With a shake of my hand I willed it to give me an answer. Holding my breath until a little negative sign came visible. My heart pounding so hard and my throat closing up I swallowed to push everything down. I wanted to run to the house and demand to talk with her, but it's going to wait for now. I hoped she wouldn't take long coming back for the answer.

My waiting for her extended to tomorrow because I stood here in front of my memories at the end of my day. There are so many pictures of her and I at competitions that the memories clogged my brain. Separating them into my favorite ones is going to be a chore, but I would enjoy each one.

8 The Taken

Thinking about Samantha at 13 years of age and how it had been when we worked hard for almost six months to prepare for The Humbold Dressage Grand Prix. The picture showed Samantha holding up her first place ribbon for the picture taker but her eyes were on me, and her smile said a thousand thanks while I stared back at her.

Before the competition I remember walking with her going over the moves and steps she and Blaze would do. She laughed hiding her fear. Making our way toward the ring she relaxed in my arm and repeated each step after me. She surprised me when she stopped and moved to stand in front of me. She reached up wrapping her arms around my neck giving me the biggest, tightest hugged. I loved it until my blood boiled under my skin. I remember rubbing my face against her head full of want and need to never let her go. The touch of her hair as it swept against my face made me want to kiss her, so I did, but on top of her head. I gave her no sign that my feelings for her were growing so deep. She released me, but I needed more. I reached for her hands taking them in mine I stared deep into those eyes as the rest of the world fell away. I wanted to give her all the strength and knowledge I had with one look.

She gave me the biggest smile I have ever seen one her face as she said, "Thank you."

I took my eyes off of her, glancing at the ring, but spoke to her, "You will be great."

Her smile enlightened my day as I hoisted her up to the saddle. Grasping my hand in her she stared down at me for the longest time. She wanted to say something, or she might want me to tell her I'd be right here waiting for her when she's done, and *for the rest of my life*, if she wanted me to. Did she have any idea that her looking at me like his killed me? No, she didn't. She rode off into the ring with poise and posture while I watched from the side.

She took first place that day a first for her. After she got her ribbon she came running and threw herself into my arms. Gently I cradled her body to mine as she wrapped her legs around me. Not in a sexual manner but as an excited young girl that cared for her trainer. With her excitement enticing mine, I held her tight and spun her around praising her every way possible.

When I let her down her body glided down mine. Full of pride down to my core I took her face in my hands. She's so happy and I wanted to share this with her, but out of the corner of my eye I saw her family on the way to congratulate her. Assuring her with a smile I turned her to face them. She ran to them with excitement while I ducked into the background of her life, taking Blaze with me as an excuse to avoid what they may have seen. Oh, that day was amazing for me. I knew then I loved this child, the problem still being she is 13 years old. Though all I wanted from Samantha at the time is to hold her hand, wrap my arms around her, and just to make her smile, it still made me feel somewhat of a pervert. She acted older and more stubborn than girls her age, but she happens to be a child and my feelings were not proper on any level. I will have to be more careful with Samantha. Not to let myself get taken with her like I did today.

9 Charish

Thinking about Samantha at 13 years of age and how it had been when we worked hard for almost six months to prepare for The Humbold Dressage Grand Prix. The picture showed Samantha holding up her first place ribbon for the picture taker but her eyes were on me, and her smile said a thousand thanks while I stared back at her.

Before the competition I remember walking with her going over the moves and steps she and Blaze would do. She laughed hiding her fear. Making our way toward the ring she relaxed in my arm and repeated each step after me. She surprised me when she stopped and moved to stand in front of me. She reached up wrapping her arms around my neck giving me the biggest, tightest hugged. I loved it until my blood boiled under my skin. I remember rubbing my face against her head full of want and need to never let her go. The touch of her hair as it swept against my face made me want to kiss her, so I did, but on top of her head. I gave her no sign that my feelings for her were growing so deep. She released me, but I needed more. I reached for her hands taking them in mine I stared deep into those eyes as the rest of the world fell away. I wanted to give her all the strength and knowledge I had with one look.

She gave me the biggest smile I have ever seen one her face as she said, "Thank you."

I took my eyes off of her, glancing at the ring, but spoke to her, "You will be great."

Her smile enlightened my day as I hoisted her up to the saddle. Grasping my hand in her she stared down at me for the longest time. She wanted to say something, or she might want me to tell her I'd be right here waiting for her when she's done, and *for the rest of my life*, if she wanted me to. Did she have any idea that her looking at me like his killed me? No, she didn't. She rode off into the ring with poise and posture while I watched from the side.

She took first place that day a first for her. After she got her ribbon she came running and threw herself into my arms. Gently I cradled her body to mine as she wrapped her legs around me. Not in a sexual manner but as an excited young girl that cared for her trainer. With her excitement enticing mine, I held her tight and spun her around praising her every way possible.

When I let her down her body glided down mine. Full of pride down to my core I took her face in my hands. She's so happy and I wanted to share this with her, but out of the corner of my eye I saw her family on the way to congratulate her. Assuring her with a smile I turned her to face them. She ran to them with excitement while I ducked into the background of her life, taking Blaze with me as an excuse to avoid what they may have seen. Oh, that day was amazing for me. I knew then I loved this child, the problem still being she is 13 years old. Though all I wanted from Samantha at the time is to hold her hand, wrap my arms around her, and just to make her smile, it still made me feel somewhat of a pervert. She acted older and more stubborn than girls her age, but she happens to be a child and my feelings were not proper on any level. I will have to be more careful with Samantha. Not to let myself get taken with her like I did today.

10 The Chosen

It was almost her birthday and her dad searched for a mare to surprise her. I went along with Kyle to make sure he was getting a good buy, and it had to be safe for Samantha. We must have looked at 36 mares before I found Daisy. Her dad's frustration with me, after each horse we did not get, elevated, but if he wanted another one for her it had to be right. Late May made it important to review all the specs of the horses we considered. Samantha would ride this one a lot over the summer, and I wanted it to meet my standards. I tried to decide if Daisy would be best for her.

The night was very warm for May so I left my door open for the fresh air to breeze into my shack. I heard a light knock, and I got up walking to the door. I smiled as I opened the door for Samantha. She walked in with confidence of a 25 year old, but went right for my memories on the shelves. One whole shelf dedicated to pictures of us together, she hesitated to pass them but glanced back at me with a grin.

If she knew what she did when she looked at me that way, she might have been more careful about coming down here for stories. I think sometimes she wants me to confess my feelings, but this time she only needed a smile before moving to the other pictures. When she picked one up in her hand she grabbed my hand leading me to the love seat where we both sat. She handed me the photo, saying, "Tell me about this one."

I started with 'Once upon a time…' as any great story would start. She smiled, giggled, and her excitement came through on her face. I went into detail about the difficult work I had put in and how many times I ended up on the ground because of that stubborn horse and his determination to not let me ride him. But I commanded him instead of leading him. That is when I learned to respect of their strength. When I gave him a little freedom he performed. She sat looking at me taking in this tale. Her eyes would get wide and then squint in disbelief. She must have had a million facial expressions that day. I took them all in to my memory bank and I enjoyed each one. The hardest part of telling her stories appeared to be when she laughed she would touch my leg. Each contact sent shots of electricity through my entire body that begged me to have her in my arms. After I shuttered the third time she asked me if she should close the door. I smirked at her not being able to tell her it's her not the cool air that drifted in the cabin. Talking her hand in mine and rubbing my thumb over her knuckles to ease my longing to pull her closer. I found this satisfying. We spent a whole night on that first picture. When I finished my story I stared into her blue eyes and grinned. She had never been this easy to please. She slouched into the couch as if exhausted from the enjoyment. Realizing how late it had gotten I stood and pulled her to her feet, "Samantha, we have to be up early, I should get you up to the house."

She huffed as I pulled her to her feet and there she stood in front of me. Almost 14 years old she took my breath away like a woman would. Smiling at her I stepped backwards toward the door, but keeping her fingers in mine. Hard to resist I held on until I got to it. Opening it I gestured for her to walk out. She did so, but I followed her. We made our way to the house without a word. I stopped at the bottom of the stairs and watched her go up the rest of the way. She hesitated at first, but hurried back down to the step above me. Her eyes meet mine and I stood there wordless gazing into them. My mouth watered and my hands got all sweaty. All I wanted to do is reach up and kiss her.

She smiled and asked, "Can I come tomorrow for another story?"

I nodded, "If your dad knows where you are."

She looked at me disappointed, but I had to make sure I would not act on my feelings. No matter how grown up she seemed she was still a child and I needed to control my desires anyway possible.

She gave me a smile and took my breath away as she hugged me so tight. Being careful I placed my arms around her letting my hands touch her briefly so I wouldn't pull her closer. She pushed away and ran up the stairs. As my gaze followed her they landed on her father standing in the doorway. He waited for her to pass by him first then gave me a nod with glaring eyes. I got an intense sensation he understood the conflict I dealt with between my head and my heart. I nodded back with understanding; No, I would not go near his daughter in any way.

11 What if

I woke to my alarm and rolled out of bed not having any sleep at all. A shower is what I needed to help me wake up this morning. Keeping the water cool shocking me awake and thankful I did. Samantha had let herself in so when I walked out of the bathroom in a towel she got a full view of a man's body. She startled me so I grabbed the sink to steady myself. I wanted to walk over to her, pull her to her feet, and wrap my arms around her taking away all the sadness that her body showed.

Her eyes were so innocent while she asked, "What did it say?"

Bracing myself for her reaction I replied, "Negative."

I didn't have to pull her to me because she got up and came to wrap her arms around my waist while her tear filled cheek rested on my chest. When her hands moved to let her fingers trail my spin the problem occurred. Standing here nearly naked with her touching me could pose as a problem if I didn't move away from her soon. It would be clear I am attracted to her by the hardness that grew beneath the towel. I tried to distract her while reaching behind me to take her hands from by body, "Samantha, that doesn't mean we are in the clear yet. It might be too early." I kissed the top of her head to prevent myself from capturing her mouth, "I need to get dress. Give me a minute so we can talk a little."

The disappointment in her face that made me hesitated. I had her hands in mine, our bodies were no longer touching, but my retreat ceased when her eyes pierced me. I wanted her bad and now, yet I let go walking away. It wasn't until I got to my room with the door closed that I could breathe.

I took my time getting dressed, almost hoping that she would run back to the house, or I would have to break down and tell her how much I loved her. It wasn't fair to her to keep this from her. She had to know what she does to me physically. She needs to be careful around me, especially if she didn't feel the same way. After getting dressed I made my way back out sitting in the chair next to her. Finding it hard to meet her eyes I asked, "If you don't want it and it still comes out you are...could you handle an abortion?"

Feeling her eyes on me I could only glance at her from the side, but enough to her shake her head no. She said she didn't want it, but that would be the only way to not have it if she was pregnant.

"Okay, then if you are, you will have it?"

This time I needed the truth of what she wanted to do so I turned to her. She still shook her head no leaving me more confused. Those are her choices. "Those would be the two options. You would have to choose one soon."

My attention on her I watched as she nodded carefully. Time is the essence, so I took a deep breath trying to collect my thoughts.

Here it goes, "If you want..." I couldn't believe I'd say this, but it came out of my mouth before thinking, "I will marry you."

Her eyes darted back to mine fiercely. The tears streamed out as she rose rushing to get away from me and out of the shack.

Had I mistaken what she wanted or needed? Did I screw up my future with Samantha? I ran my hands through my hair wondering if I should go to the house and force her to tell me what she wants me to do. No, pushing her to include me would be a mistake. She didn't want me or what I offered. I over stepped my grounds with her and her family. Shit, now what should I do?

Lost on what to do I head out to start my daily routine. Still early enough the sun hadn't risen. Going over in my head what I had tried to talk to her about but nothing resolved. Except for my understanding she didn't want the baby, and she didn't want me. Hurt and upset the sadness filled me as I started my daily chores. Dreaming about my stubborn little Samantha, growing more pissed as the day grew strong. My mind drifted to the multiple times she had told me I did everything wrong. The thing is when you are angry you can get a lot more done.

I skipped breakfast and kept working. I wanted to blow off steam, but it grew deep within me as my mind wandered off to think about all the things she does to entice my feelings. When this calmed down I will point out what a tease is and explain to her how not to be one because if she knew what one was maybe she wouldn't be in this mess.

All the ranting voices in my head came to a halt when I saw Kyle walking into the barn. He followed me for a while and then gave me a hand. He wanted to ask me something, but hesitated. I continued with my work and he continued to help me. Nervousness crept in with him hanging around waiting for the right moment. The only time he has ever hung out with me was when he had concerns about Sam's behavior. My instincts justified when he asked, "So, do you know what is up with Sam?"

I looked at him and tried to keep a blank face, "No, is there something wrong?"

His eyes searched my face for any nervous twitch, but I tried to not show him my concern with just the mention of her name.

"Yes, she didn't come down for breakfast and I noted she hasn't been down all week to help you. She always comes down to spend as much time with the horses she can."

I shook my head and went back to work, "If there's something wrong wouldn't she have told you?" He would realize that I'm lying to him if he'd see my eyes. Not wanting to lie to him, but I also didn't want to betray Samantha's trust. It seemed pointless if she's not pregnant.

He made me more nervous as he expressed another point, "You didn't come in for breakfast either."

"Nope, I just ate a bowl of cereal. I had plans for cleaning the stalls today. Sometimes you feed me to well and then I can't move."

He chuckled with this, "Do you want her to come help you today?"

"If she wants to, I enjoy her company even though she will point out everything I'm doing wrong." I looked up at him chuckling to myself. Knowing I was right, and the light conversation, his curiosity had subsided. He left me to my work, and relief filled me with his exit. I sat down on a bale of hay to sort this out. There wouldn't be anything to figure out if she wasn't pregnant.

I went back to work, hoping my frustrations would subside this time. She adventured back down to help with the chores. I detected her watching me from the gate, but she is still sullen.

"Are you okay?"

She nodded and gave me a slight smiled.

"Are you going to stand there and watch or are you going to help me?"

She came in and worked to help me with the stalls. We finished the first couple of stalls not speaking. By the third stall the silence echoed in my ears. I threw hay at her just to hear her. She giggled and tossed hay back at me. We continued to goof off until we finished another one. When I moved to the next one she disappeared. Not prying I went back to work, but when I completed the fourth one, and she didn't reappear, I went searching for her. I found her in with Blaze talking and hugging him. Satisfied I let her have private time. Sometimes saying things out loud you can find the answer. She came back, and we got a few more done. On the last one Samantha became playful. She shoved hay down my shirt and I grabbed her falling on top of her in a large pile of it.

The curves of a woman's body beneath mine caused a bodily reaction I enjoyed. I stared into her eyes. My body enticed by the mounds and valleys of her under me. I traced my hand along her cheek, "I am serious, Samantha. I will marry you and take care of you."

She shook her head, "Not if you don't love me. I won't ask you to do that."

The need to press my lips against hers is unbearable. To lick those lips and taste her, "I love you. You know that."

She shook her head again, "You don't. Not in the right way and it wouldn't be enough."

Pressing my lips to her forehead, refraining from caressing her lips from mine, I mouthed to her, "But I will do whatever you need. We would be happy here together, and you could do whatever you want. Go to school, not go to school. It wouldn't matter because I'd take care of you."

She ran her hands up my back and my body stiffened as my want for her grew. She kissed me under my chin sending an alarm to my brain. I pushed up and away from her, afraid that I would take advantage of her right there. I liked the way her fingers stroked my back, the way her eyes penetrated my soul, and that mouth tempted me with a soft kiss, it was all too much. She's 16 years of age and I'm 24. It would not be proper to act on my desires when she is thoroughly confused. She had to make decisions that would be best for her based on what she would go through. I stood up and pulled her to her feet. She looked at me with a glance and I went back to work.

She took me by surprise when she yelled at me, "That is what I mean; not enough." She stormed from the stall. I tried to follow, but she was so quick to get away from me. I should have just told her that my feelings were deep. They ran deeper than she'd ever guessed. I should have told her I had been in love with her for years. How was I going to make this right?

At dinner time I went to the house. I needed to speak to her. I needed to make her understand. She didn't come down to dinner. I waited and ate slowly, but there was no hope of seeing her. My heart hurt as I went back to my shack and forced myself to get sleep.

12 *The Apple*

My memories of the pictures brought me back to the next time she came for a story. Her parents gone for the weekend so she took the opportunity to come down for more stories. She handed me another picture as I sat on the love seat. I moved over to give her room. "I am 16 years old in this one."

She giggled as she gazed at the framed photo, "You were cute."

I took the famed photo back and took a good look at myself. I wish I was that age now, Samantha would be my girlfriend. Laughing at myself over how pathetic I had been. So young at 14 years of age, Samantha sits on my couch resembling a grown woman. I told the story behind the image. She smiled and listened without a word. She sat there for hours holding my framed memory and listening to my story about my responsibility for one horse. Part of my development on working with horses started here. No matter what I did this horse did not like me. I walked and talked to him every day trying to win his trust so I could ride him. Everything I did had a backwards effect causing me frustration. It had been months before I found the secret of winning him over to my control. Samantha, impatient to hear what the final secret could be, she blurted, "So why did he let you ride him."

Dragging the time out trying to spend more with her, no longer prolonging the inevitable I admitted that the horse showed me the answer.

I went down with an apple in the morning, but kept it in my pocket. This stupid horse changed, now tentative and responsive. He wouldn't stop nudging me and rubbing his face to my chest. With his behavior I decided I would try riding him again. When I got on he didn't like it, but he allowed me to work with him a little. He tolerated me and I thought I accomplished this great task that took six months to do.

It wasn't until I cooled him down and groomed him that the horse nibbled on my pocket. I pushed him away, and he continued to be persistent on getting that apple from me. I pulled out the apple and his head followed every which way I held it. That is what he wanted the whole time. I ran from him and he pranced behind me pushing me with his nose. He pursued me all over and I enjoyed the controlled. I gave him the apple making him my new best friend. Finding him every day full of anticipation satisfied the sense of my training ability. He allowed me to do everything I wanted as long as I carried an apple in my pocket. I learned to wait until the end of the day to give him the apple in order for him to respond to my every wish.

She giggled with this story while she curled up on the loveseat putting her head in my lap as I explained every detail. I wanted to make this last all night. This was the most comfortable she made herself been with me and I was just talking to her. My desires filled having her near me. Making the story so long she grew tired of and fell asleep. I sat there holding this child as she slept. Keeping her here is not a choice but while I allowed it I took advantage of adoring her. Her long hair resembled silk as I ran my fingers through it, her eyelashes dark against her skin, and those lips a natural tone of pink, and so deliciously tempting that I decided that it's time to give in and carry her to the house. Tracy met me in the living room and I laid down my sweet Samantha on the couch.

"You know you could take her to her room. We all know you care for her over me."

That was the first time her sister said anything to me. I have spent no time with Tracy. She is too high and mighty for wasting her time on me, or anyone else that worked here. I carried my sweet Samantha up to her room as Tracy directed me in to the right door. I laid her in her bed, but looked around her room. There were charts and posters on horses; every muscle, every bone, and every breed of horse. She had somewhere in the neighborhood of one hundred plastic molded horse statues. She loved them as much as I thought she had. I tucked her in and kissed my hand and placed it on her *forehead. I went to leave her room, but Tracy stood there watching me, "Why do you feel that way about her? She is a child."*

I walked past her mumbling, "And so are you."

13 Apparently

In reality Tracy's jealousy caused this whole mess with Samantha. When Tracy tried to kiss me, Samantha assumed I returned the encounter with feelings. If she had a clue of where my heart belonged, she wouldn't have even looked at my nephew, let alone do that with him. With new determination I'd do something about *that*... tomorrow.

Anticipation of seeing Samantha made my night sleepless. I will tell her how my gut turns when she hurts, how when she's close my body tenses, and how her eyes dig deep into my soul. Serious about wanting to take care of her the rest of her life, I hoped she would understand this to be the truth, not something I would lie about. Rising from bed with a new purpose I got dressed fast, I did the morning routine, and then headed up for breakfast. It is time to come out about my state of mind. When she didn't come down my insides tormented me with devastation. I needed to talk to her before she made anymore decisions that didn't include me. This morning wasn't the only place I experienced her absence; I didn't get to see her the whole day.

Having a hard time sleeping again, I rolled over realizing that she consumed me day and night. I put my hand to my chest to find my heart racing with wanting to tell her the truth. Rolling over to stomach it convulsed with knotting and twisting. Oh, what this child does to my heart.

Giving up on sleeping I got up and headed out to start my day.

I made it through the morning hours without breakfast. Forcing myself to eat a sandwich I opted to eat in my cabin so I could go back to work without being distracted by the thought of Samantha. Still no word from Sam I took out a new mare out to work with her for a while and found her well behaved. Doing a cool down with the hose and then grooming her helped me to escape my brain. Involved in my work intensely, the only distraction came with Samantha's voice yelling for me.

The screaming hinted at madness. Samantha's voice at a new pitch shrieking my name over and over again caused me to panic. Is she okay, does she need me beyond reason, or did she want me to take care of her? I tried to hurry to tie the mare up, so I could settle my suffering of hearing her screams. As I stepped out the door of the wash room her body hit me full force wrapping every inch of her around me. She clung to my body, her face at my neck, her arms around my neck, but she didn't elaborate so I held her.

Her emotions made me want to throw up. The warmth of her breath panting against my skin I closed my eyes with anticipation.

Her whisper flowed into my ear, "Kam, I'm not."

My breath hitched forgetting to exhale as I squeezed her tighter. Even though its good news, being in my arms for far too long is not. My mind went blank.

She kissed my ear, my neck, and then my cheek. Oh shit her mouth hit mine hard and forceful. I stood stiff and scared of wanting to kiss her. No, I shouldn't, but she is here in my arms and I had every intention of telling her how everything about her did it for me on a level so deep I couldn't explain *it*. Should I confess if she isn't pregnant? I move my lips to hers once watching her face. Her eyes met mine while her lips moved to mine again. I closed my eyes and gave her the emotions within me with my next kiss. Tilting my head a little moving deeper, savoring the sweetness, her taste mimicked her scent. My hands held her back to keep her against me as we continued to exchange our affections. She grasped my face and stopped kissing me to look at me in the eyes.

Confusion danced with her expression and I remained dumbfounded on what to do or say. She took that responsibility away from me when she spoke, "Kam?" her voice reflected her need of answers. No longer able to refuse my inner desires I closed my eyes and nodded.

Her quiet whisper traced my lips, "Are you sure?"

My kiss wasn't as convincing enough? Gripping her body tighter to mine I immersed myself into her pressing, sucking, nibbling anything to give her a better idea of what I sought. If I already made a mistake I needed to make sure she understood my deepest aspiration.

She pulled away from the kiss not my arms. She was panting almost as hard as me. Resting my forehead to hers to regain my sanity, she did the same. When a cunning grin grew on her face, her eyes came back to meet mine. Breathy she gasped, "Holy Cow!"

We laughed together for a moment until she slid from my grip. She grabbed my hand leading me back into the wash room. Slowly releasing me from her grasped I slowed to a linger waiting to see what she'd do or say. Pacing back and forth with her fingers to her lips with a quirky smile hidden; she seemed to process everything that had just happen. Finally she came to a halt, glanced at me, and the biggest grin swept across her face. The next thing I knew she was in my arms again. I wanted to kiss her again, but opted to kiss the top of her head. Her heart beating almost as hard as mine, I held her to help calm us both.

Her voice trembled, "Kam, thank you so much."

I didn't understand why she thanked me. This is not a good thing. I'm astonished that I kissed and then admitted that I felt this way. It will come back to bite me in the ass. She slid from my arms, picked up the brushes, and groomed the horse I had been working on. She moved around her glancing back at me, but then continued to take care of the grooming.

"Kam, I will enter that contest you told my dad about."

Not taking my eyes off of her I waited for her to elaborate.

"We would have to work hard because I haven't done a contest in a long time."

When she groomed a horse she glides as if she were dancing. Catching me staring at her she continued, "We will have to spend a lot of time together."

Not able to speak a word I nodded.

"It has to be a lot of time. I wouldn't be happy if I didn't take first place."

Her glance came back at me until our eyes met once again.

I agreed with a nod, again.

"Do you have time to help me? I mean a lot of time to get rid of all my bad habits'?"

I'm in so much trouble here. If I spend more time with her it will be more torture because I cannot let that happen again for a long time.

Her hands continued to brush and trace over the mare. Goose bumps rose on my skin with the thought of her touching me. Standing there dumbfounded awaiting her conclusion. My fantasy of kissing her again filled my brain, but her look showed her confusion by my reaction to her. I wanted to scream I loved her, but my voice remained silent. I studied her as she made her way around the horse. When she approached the same side as me she made her way closer and handed me the brushes. I took them, but didn't take my eyes from her. She smiled, "Good, we will start today."

That's all I could ask for, more time with her. A lot more time to be alone with her to torment my wish to have her.

"What time?" She asked as if I have a choice in the matter.

I shrugged my shoulders waiting for her to tell me. She reached up with her fingers and touched my lips, "After dinner?"

I nodded, but my body reacted to her movement and my hand came to hold hers fingertips to my lips harder. I closed my eyes and kissed her fingers that touched me there. Hoping this would never end I refused to leave my dream. When she slipped from me I awakened to her soft caring smile as she backed away from me. Turning she took off out of the wash room and up toward the house running. I stepped out to watch her run from me. *What the hell did I just do?*

"Kam, what's *that* about?"

I almost dropped dead when Kyle ask me that. I turned and headed back in the grooming room, "She decided to compete. The one I told you about."

He followed me in, "Really? She seemed excited."

"Yeah, I guess. She wants to train today after dinner."

He chuckled, "Could that be why she seemed depressed. She hasn't worked towards something in a long time."

I went back to grooming the horse I had been working with. Kyle followed me. If he sensed the excitement in her did he realize we kissed? Confusion ran wild in my brain on what I should say. My heart pounding fast and hard making it difficult to have eyed contact with him, it would be apparent in my eyes.

"Did she say what horse she wants to use?"

"No, I guess she will tell me that later."

"Do you have time for this?"

"Yeah, I guess I will make time. She is better now and if that will help... yeah, I will do it."

"Good. If you need help with anything else because you're busy with her, let me know. I may have to get you help."

"Thank you."

"No. Thank you, Kamron. It's nice to see her happy again. You're sure you don't know what happened?"

I stopped grooming the mare swallowed hard to confess a small part of the story, "It might have something to do with my nephew, but I sent him home."

He gave me a slight grin, "I thought the same thing."

"He won't be a problem anymore."

"I think she liked him."

I made my way around him to bring the mare to her stall, "Yeah, I do, but he's not good for her. He will not be a problem again."

Kyle followed me and closed the gate behind me so when I tried to go out he stood in the way. Shit, he's trying to get me to confess kissing his daughter?

"Kam, you are part of this family. It's not right you wouldn't have him here. Just, next time, keep a closer watch on him."

I nodded as he opened the gate for me, "Is there anything else? I need to get stuff done if I am helping Samantha later."

He grinned and pat me on the back, "No, but I wouldn't know what to do without you."

I chuckled feeling a little guilty as he walked away, and I went back to work.

14 Grey

Instead of going up for dinner I made a list of items to be done for Samantha to be ready. Show jumping didn't mean the horse does all the work. Planning a fitness regimen for her; she isn't a little girl anymore and the weight difference had to be backed with skill on how to use her body more. As things came to mind I wrote them down in a list. The list grew with thoughts of being prepared and what we would do to achieve it.

It seemed more difficult to make a list for the horse because I didn't want to assume which one she would ride. I wanted her to use Grey. He's a beautiful specimen with a lot of potential but hasn't done this competitive activity. He's new to the stable, bought for Tracy, but she spent no time with him. If I start now he'd be ready in time for the competition. He's young and trusting enough we could get him to try anything. Knowing that if I talked to Kyle he would agree with me, but I didn't know what this would do to Samantha or Tracy.

I walked up to the house hoping their dinner time had ended, but they all remained sitting at the table. Entering the dining room just in time for desert, I avoided looking at Samantha. I wouldn't allow myself to be distracted if its what she wanted.

While I tried to get enough gumption to ask about Grey, they continued their dinner conversation. When Kyle asked me a question it startled me because I hadn't been paying attention to what they talked about.

He laughed, "I can see you are preoccupied. Would you like to share?"

I nodded and stood up walking around the table, pacing. I stopped and looked at Sam, "Did you decide on which horse you would like to enter the contest with?"

She frowned at me, "Blaze."

I shook my head, "Sam, he hasn't trained since the last competition. With his age we should consider all of them before you decide."

She glared at me, "What are you talking about?"

"Well, if you want to take first place it should be one that hasn't wiped out, hit a pole, stumbled, or has fear. He just has seen too much and I am afraid he will spook."

"Not with you training him. You are amazing and I have complete confidence in you."

Grimacing, I glanced at Kyle for some help with convincing her. He leaned back in his chair with his arms folded across his chest, "Which one are you suggesting?"

"One of the horses that we have not competed with yet."

Sam stood up, "Why. Blaze has done amazing for me."

"Yes, but you want to win, right?"

She stomped her foot at me disagreeing.

Kyle asked his wife, "Well, momma, what's your decision?"

Raquel, Kyle's wife and mother to Samantha and Tracy, never said much but she's Kyle's love. He loved her and worshiped the ground she walked on. She's hard to read, because she is so sweet most of the time, but also she's the iron behind the curtain.

Taking her time she appraised Sam and then me before she asked, "Which horse would you choose?"

Given the opportunity I suggested, "Grey."

Tracy had a hissy fit. Saying that Grey's hers and if he's competing it should be her that trains with him. I saw her on him twice since we got him. Hell, I rode him more than she did.

Wanting a chance to explain I continued, "Look, Sam is the best rider and you know it. Grey has the potential of winning. He doesn't scare easily and he would push it to the next level."

Raquel stood up, "Kamron, I am sorry. Both my girls do not agree. Though we trust your judgment, we also have faith in your ability. If Sam wants to ride Blaze, then that is how it will be."

She took her plate heading to the kitchen. Shocked that she decided so blatantly; my eyes followed her until they fell on Sam. The tears already welling up in her eyes, she confirmed what she felt, "It has to be Blaze."

Not intending on causing a huge scene I nodded with understanding. Tracy got up to go to the kitchen mumbling, "She gets all the attention."

Wanting Kyle to smooth everything over I gestured to him, but he just shrugged. When Sam stormed off too I lost the argument. I sat back down to finish my desert. He leaned to the table. "You are right, but sometimes we need to give into them. They feel important when you let them decide and this will show Samantha you know best."

"But, Sam could win this year. We are starting early and if we..."

Already shaking his head he interrupted me, "If it's meant to be then it will happen. Otherwise, I am expecting you to do your best."

I figured with Sam being angry with me for bringing up the issue at hand, we wouldn't start today. When I got back to the shack I went to work on a game plan for training Blaze, not having a choice.

A knock on my door came loud and clear as Sam entered without me getting up. I cracked a smile as she walked to the table and sat down. I continued to look at my plan of action for the both of them.

"Kam, I'm sorry I should listen to you."

I looked up at her. Did she admit that she's wrong? "So, you'll ride Grey?"

She shook her head, "No, I trust Blaze."

I nodded and handed her workout list.

"What is this for?"

"You."

"Why do I need to work out?"

"Blaze is getting older and you're not a little girl anymore."

She smiled big with this, "But, you'll make me do this?"

"Yes, I will do it with you."

That made her happy. She stood up and walked behind me. My body went tense with awareness of her, nervous about what was going on in the mind of hers.

She rubbed my shoulders, "You are amazing Kam, and I have faith in you. If anyone can train Blaze it's you."

I chuckled again and shook my head, "You realize how hard it will be. You need to be light as a feather and compliment his moves."

She traced her hands down my arms moving her face close to mine, "You are amazing and I am confident you can make this happen. What time in the morning?"

I grinned, "If I remember, a little girl once told me we start at 5 am around here."

She kissed my cheek and moved away from me towards the door, "I will have my running shoes on."

I laughed out loud as she took off for the house. She will drive me crazy on purpose.

I lay in my bed pondering what will happen with my little angle now. She's not pregnant, and she understood my feelings for her; I wished that she didn't want Blaze for this competition. Not that he is old or anything, but he is edgy of new tricks. I had to try again tomorrow to talk her out of using him. It's a bad idea when weighing all aspects of what they are required to do, so I need to make that clear. She was grasping at straws to keep Blaze a winner. I drifted off thinking about her stubborn pout and how I wanted to consume it with my mouth. Wondering if a nibbling or sucking would make it disappear. Yes, that would make her smile instead of pouting.

15 The Instinct

I laughed at her stomping her feet when she didn't get the horse, but there seemed to be issues that didn't give me impression that he'd be a wise choice. He didn't like when I touched his legs. He moved away from me when I felt his stomach. She only wanted him because he's a stallion with a black shinny coat. I kept testing him and I advised her dad that he would be unsafe for her. Determined that she could handle it, she irritated me with her insistence. At 13 years of age, the mindset of a 20 year old, she protested my disagreeing with her. She pointed out all the good things, and I indicated all the bad. Satisfied that Kyle decided to go with my decision. I promised to find her another one, but she insisted getting this one so she didn't talk to me for two weeks.

When I told her I will compromise my own instincts and call to see if they still had him. She jumped up and down in front of me, "When can we get him?"

I held up my finger to hold her off for a minute to listen to what the seller told me.

"I need him today. Kam, tell me what we need to do to get him."

I hung up the phone shaking my head. She was mad all over again, "They sold him and it's your fault. He should be mine, but you had to be stubborn, bossy, and big jerk."

I finally put my hand over her mouth to shut her up. Kyle walked in laughing, "What is she doing now?"

"She is angry with me about the stallion but when I just called them…" I looked at her in the eyes, "I found they had to put him down. His insides were all twisted beyond repair. He would cost us a bundle and then he still would have had to be put down."

Her blue eyes looked transparent as they filled with tears, "Why are you right all the time?"

I hated that I am right about this one, but she'd se I am looking out for her, and her family. I wasn't trying to torture her by not giving into her whims. Acting her age again she stormed off angry. She isn't going to speak to me for a long time. It's her way of winning an argument.

16 Immaturity

The ache in my chest reminding me what happens to me when I let her down. I hated being right about the stallion because I would have loved to seen her on him. She holds herself so strong and straight and with his handsome statue it would have made her... unforgettable.

Her immaturity bothered me, but I have to face facts. No matter how she looks she is still a child in so many other ways. Finding it challenging to put up with the pouts, the whining, and the teary eyes made me want to take her over my knee to knock sense into her, but I am not her father.

I hadn't given it much thought until now, how did he deal with her when she acts like that? He probably gave into her every chance he could; she was adorable when those blue eyes spilled out the tears.

I got up and walked out to the living room. Not being able to get Sam off my mind, I went to look over my pictures again. There's something about her that made her more beautiful when she didn't put on a face like the other girls especially Tracy. Maybe that's why I found her so breath taking, she hardly ever wears makeup.

I pulled one of the pictures off the shelf, from the time when we held an auction here at the ranch. It had been more work than I planned on, but Kyle did make out that day. We got Timber, a 3 year old stud, Pearl, a white 2 year old mare, and the pony. Samantha decided to call him Patches due to him being a painted pinto. I sat down remembering the day and how pushy she happened to be at 15 about all the horses she wanted.

Horse Play

17 The Picks

"Kam, did you check them over yet? I already picked out the ones I want."

"Samantha, I am a little busy organizing..."

"Okay, so there's one, a stud. He is 17 hands, strong Kam, real strong. His legs are good, no swelling, and no joint issues."

"Samantha!"

"Second, is Pearl, and she looks like a gem Kam. She is a quarter horse all white. Have you ever seen such a thing? Anyway... she is a beauty. I think dad can bread her with..."

"SAMANTHA!"

She stomped at me to hush me, and kept after me, "Kam, fine. But the one I want, really, really, really want is this painted pony. I already named him and he nuzzles. It's not like I didn't check him over either, but this one would be for me. Just for me to enjoy riding. We connect, Kam, I can sense it. He is supposed to be mine."

"S A - M A N - T H A!"

She put her hand u because she didn't want to hear any excuses. Shaking my head and pushed her away from me, but she wouldn't leave me alone until I looked at the ones she wanted.

Yelling at her with the intention of making her see how busy I am, "If you help me I can get to it sooner!"

I knew she was serious when she did just that. She groomed three horses, filled water buckets, and she helped me hand out bidding number.

A last minute announcement I delayed the bidding by an hour so I could check out the horses she wanted me to evaluate. Kyle seemed pleased that I felt strong enough to make a quick decision making his daughter happy.

She led me to seven different horses telling me what she liked and what she didn't. I gave each of them a once and twice over and decided that Kyle should at least look at three of them, which were Samantha's favorite three. Any of them would be good to have here on the ranch and if we got the pony I would be busy; a little job security and satisfaction for me. Training a pony is easier than training an old stubborn horse. She went to her father with the three I had picked, and to my surprise he purchased all three. The picture I held displayed her with all of them. The gleam in her eye priceless and I understood why he bought them. She was irresistible when she wanted something bad enough.

18 Confessions

I put the picture back on my shelf and went to bed. I closed my eyes but I saw the excitement in her eyes that day and it melted my heart. After we set them up in stalls she gave me the biggest hug telling me that I'm not that bad anymore. Her moods varied up and down when it came to me; one minute sweet as pie and the other so angry with me that she wouldn't even talk to me. I still don't understand how I fell in love with her. I think it was everything about her, but most of all her passion for these horses. That is the only thing we both agree on entirely.

I got up in the morning putting cut off sweats on, my old tennis shoes that I forgotten that I even owned, and a muscle shirt. If I'm running I need to be comfortable. I headed up to the house a little after 5 am. Sitting on the step waiting for me with her pink and blue Nike attire and matching shoes, Sam seemed patient. I shook my head as I walked to her.

"I thought you said 5 am."

"Yeah, I got up at 5."

"I have been waiting."

"Fine, let's go." Glad I had her get up early for this, not; I was finding her difficult already. We started with a light jog and she kept up with me no problem. We ran the fence line of the driveway and then out the gate and down the main road. We didn't talk but with jogging it wouldn't be easy. We started with two miles and when we got back I went straight for the hose for a drink and then fell to my back. She stood there not straining at all, "Are you getting too old for this?"

I raised my eyebrows thinking I am too old for *her*.

I dragged myself up to go do my morning chores and she helped until we got to the dirty stuff and then she bailed on me. She wasn't dressed for this type of work.

"When should I come back?"

"How about we start weight lifting at three this afternoon?"

She nodded and jogged to the house and I let my gut out. This sucked. I am so out of shape it wasn't funny, and I'm supposed to be training her.

When she came back we started on strength and conditioning. We did sit ups, pushups, and some other things I had put down. She didn't have problem doing any of it and I struggled shortly after starting. How can I work like I do and be this out of shape? I had muscles everywhere already so why did this hurt so bad? Am I becoming soft and old? How could she kiss me like that if I am as bad off as I feel?

Dinner time she went to the house and I went to do my evening chores. Knowing it would take me longer with how soar I am. Kyle came down and gave me a hand. He was laughing at me because I groaned with every movement.

Days and weeks went by quickly and I hadn't worked with Blaze at all but exercising didn't hurt as bad anymore. We were going to start working with Blaze today. He had to build that trust issue again, because it had been so long. We stayed in the riding rink but I didn't put a saddle on him. I wanted her to be connected to his movements. She was directing him with the reins again and I reminded her of the light touch that he respected from her. She loosened her grip and let the reins fall over her hands. She was doing well so I wanted to push it further.

"Sam, when you want him to go left squeeze your left leg and pull it back a little and use the reins lightly so he understands."

"What?"

"I want him to feel your movements without the reins. Complete trust."

She tried but he wasn't responding. I got up with her and took her hands with the reins, "When I pull on your leg move your hand like this."

She nodded. I put my hand on her thigh and closed my eyes to endure my desires. I took her leg pulling it back a little and pushed it to him, "Squeeze your leg muscle and turn him."

She did and he got it.

"Now try the other way."

She let him walk a ways and she did the other way. I felt her leg move that way it was supposed to without me touching her. He followed her lead. We did this for almost an hour.

"Now, Sam try it without pulling the reins."

She did and it works. She was so pleased with herself, "So, how is this supposed to help him?"

He will be able to read your body. She leaned back into me.

"Kam, my birthday is coming up."

"Don't tell me you want a different horse. He is getting it."

"No, there is only one thing I really want."

"Did you tell your dad? I am sure he will get you whatever you want."

"This is something that he can't give me."

"So, you want me to get it for you?"

"Yes."

"What is it?"

She turned to me a little, "I want you to kiss me again."

I closed my eyes and traced my face along hers whispering to her, "I can't and it's not fair to ask this of me."

"Why... I mean... can't you?"

"You'll only be 17, I am still 24."

"So it's because I'm jail bait."

I laughed with a sigh, "Yes."

She sat up more and started to make him jog around the rink. I pulled the reins for him to stop and slid off, "If you're going to make him run it would be better without the extra weight."

She huffed and took off yelling, "I still want that for my birthday gift. It's the only thing I want."

I walked to the gate ignoring her as Kyle walked up, "So what does she want for her birthday."

She was going to get me into trouble this little girl. I shook my head, "Something I can't get for her."

"Tell me and I will get it. We can say it's from you."

I laughed out loud, "No, I will get her something I can afford on my own, but thank you for the offer."

"She really looks up to you. You don't put up with her shenanigans."

I watched her ride around the ring her back perfectly straight and her lead so gentle. She rode up to us, "Dad, do you want to see something really cool that Kam taught me just now."

He climbed up the fence and sat down, "I would love to."

She went to the other side and laid the reins down and nudged him and he started to walk. When he got a little further I could tell she was directing him to turn, but he wasn't. She yelled at me, "Did you do something so it worked before, because he isn't doing it."

"Sam, calm down and take your time. Relax and don't push it."

She went further and tried again and this time it work. She was riding around the rink in complete bliss. I chuckled and Kyle looked at me, "So, this will help her with the competition?"

"Yes, with Blaze being older I am worried that he'll get spooked. If he trusts her this way he will know that she can led him safely."

He nodded and went back to watching Sam.

"I have some chores; tell her to come find me when she is done playing with Blaze. I'll help her cool him down."

When she finally came in I was shoveling out a stall and putting feed in getting it ready for Blaze. She walked him to the grooming room and I followed. She was hosing him down and I stood to watched her. She wasn't looking at me, but I could see that little smirk of a smile as she moved around him.

"So, what is next?"

"Small jumps."

"No with him, with us?"

"No us."

She glared at me, "Do you have feelings for me or not."

I didn't say or do anything. It was wrong to tell her I did and wrong for her to ask me that. I also didn't want to lie and hurt her. She turned off the hose and took the brush and started to groom him. I walked over and grabbed another one and started on the other side. He was getting spooked, "Sam, knock it off."

"What? I'm not doing anything."

I glared at her over him and that smirk was still there.

"Remember the second day when we went up to the house and were washing together."

I looked over Blaze at her wondering where this was going.

"That's when I knew."

"Knew what?"

"That you are my soul mate. You are absolutely perfect. We love the same things and you knew more than me. How could I not fall in love with you?"

"At 11 Sam? That is what you call a crush."

She moved to his neck and was more careful and she peeked under his chin, "When did you start to feel things?"

I moved closer to her to talk more quietly, "I don't want to say."

She gave me that nasty glare again.

"Sam, it's wrong. I can't no matter how I feel. It's not right."

She stormed out and I knew she was angry with me. How can I not do this without hurting her? She walked back in around the side I was on. She traced her hand along my back as she passed me. I closed my eyes as I felt the heat rush to her touch. She stopped in front of Blaze handing him a carrot. I had to chuckle because she never use to give them treats until I made it okay for her to do that. I smiled and shook my head.

"What?"

"You're only doing that because... nothing."

"Yes, so, I remember the stories too."

We continued to take care of Blaze and walked him back to the stall. She walked in with him and he nuzzled his nose to her. I waited by the gate. She walked out and looked up at me, "Tell me when."

I lowered my face, "Probably around 13."

She grinned at me with that little smirk, "That long?"

I nodded.

"How come you didn't tell me?"

"I can't do this, Sam."

"We're not doing anything, Kam. I just wish I would have known."

"Why, then you wouldn't have been yourself. I like you the way you are."

Kyle walked up, "We all like you the way you are, Sam. Is there something going on at school, or with your friends that you don't feel good about yourself?"

I just about shit my pants. He is worried about her for him to check on her this much. All this was such bad timing.

19 Surprises

We continued to work every day. Sometimes I would ride with her, but most of the time I made her do stuff on her own. She is such a natural at all the performance riding. Now that I'm physically fit and not winded every time I ran made it easier to work with Blaze. He did the jumps on a lead first, then she'd come down and they'd do a few together. Everything progressed the way I hoped it would. Increasing the difficulty of the jumps Blaze continued to improve without getting spooked at all.

Her birthday came much sooner than I realized. I picked up a new saddle for her. Thank god I tucked as much money as I did, away. This new saddle almost put me at broke. Her family had plans for a nice dinner at home early and friends at 9 pm. They rented a huge tent and had a DJ coming.

Before dinner I went up to get her. Wanting to surprise her I put a blindfold over her eyes and lead her to the stables. Kyle, Raquel, and Tracy all followed down to take pictures of the gift. Another picture for my shelf is what I hoped for. Standing in front of her I tried to quiet the gasps of astonishment. As I took off the blind fold she walked forward staring at the saddle. At first she said nothing clearly she hated it, but then she traced her hand over every inch, pulled up the stirrups, and then read the tag, "You did not get this for me?"

Good it surprised her. "Yes, it's all yours."

"But it's a Pessoa A/O. It's too much."

The smile on my face must have matched the rest of the families. Kyle nudged me, "You should have told me. That's quiet the gift and we could've helped out."

Shaking my head no, because I wanted this to be from me to her, something the two of us can share. Reinforcing it's my gift to her I explained, "It's for the competition you will win." Directing my comment to Sam, "You will have this saddle for a long time and it's something I see you looking at all the time."

She glared at me over the top of it, "I can't believe you did this." But her voice did not sound happy. Her tone was filled with hurt and disappointment.

"What? You don't like it?"

Her eyes met mine showing me how disappointed she is. When her eyes wandered over her family before they came back I worried she'd tell me why she didn't want the saddle as her gift, but she didn't. The only thing she said is, "It's too much."

She took off running all the way to the house. That isn't the reaction I had expected. Glancing at Kyle wishing he'd tell me what I just did that made her cry. Deep down I wondered if this had to do with the kiss she asked me for, but she has to understand that we can't do that again. She is still too young for me even at 17 years old. Raquel walked up patting my arm, "The saddle is a beautiful gift. It might have been a little much and you know how girls can be emotional. Maybe she didn't realize you cared about her that much."

What did she mean that much? She's the only one in the family I spent any time with. I care about her that much. She's been a huge part of my life for the last six years, and will be for the rest of our lives if she'll have me. Standing there dumfounded wondering what I should do now. That is the best gift I've ever given someone, and it made her cry. Kyle patted my back as Raquel pulled Tracy from the stable with her mouth hanging open.

Fear of what Samantha will do I asked Kyle, "Did I do something wrong?"

He shook his head, "Like momma said, girls are emotional. Come up and have cake with us."

Not wanting to see her I shook my head. My heart hurt after she reacted that way. I suppose I could return it, but she would look so good on it. Dam her for being a spoiled brat, "I'll take the night off if you don't mind."

He nodded and walked up to the house. Taking my broken heart back to the shack to sulk I left the saddle on the wood horse. Laying down in bed the anger seeped into my head. How could I ever think I loved someone who is so stubborn, irritating, and spoiled?

My mind drifted to the day she brought me to meet Carmel.

Horse Play

20 The Caramel

She came running into my shack without knocking or anything pulling me from my bed. I grabbed a T-shirt as I ran out the door following her.

"Something is wrong with Carmel. He is hacking up a lung and getting sick."

"Okay."

I followed her down to the barn and sure enough he was sick.

"Do something. You know everything. Do something for him."

I picked up the phone in the stables and called for the Vet. This is way over my head.

We stayed with him and I ran my hand over his stomach trying to figure out what made him so sick. I checked his teeth and there was brown stuff all over them.

Samantha is close to hyperventilating with worry begging me to help him. I had seen nothing like this before. I tried to get him to drink but he wouldn't. He just kept hacking. I lead him to the grooming area because there's more room for the Vet to work on him. I heard him pull in, "Sam, go show him where we are."

She ran from me as I traced my hands over his stomach again. His stomach heaved to trying to get rid of what had made him sick. The Vet walked in and looked him over. He hesitated as he gestured to Sam, "She needs to..."

Getting it I tried to push her out, "Sam, you should go get your dad."

In her whinny voice she cried, "I can't leave him. If he dies I won't be able to say goodbye."

I picked her up and carried her out of the grooming area and shut the door, "Sam, if he dies I don't want you to watch."

She's angry with me, but called the house from the stable phone. I held my hand out to stop her from going back in when Kyle showed up. Kyle didn't even have to ask, but he did anyway, "Please keep her out."

I felt so bad that I couldn't help him and I couldn't calm her. It was the worst feeling in the world. She shouldn't care this much about an animal.

"Sam, how did you know he's sick?"

"I walked down here to say good night."

"Do you do that often?"

"Yes, every night. Can't you do something?"

"No, I'm not sure what the problem is."

Kyle opened the door, "Kam, we need your help."

"Sam, for the life of me... stay out."

Her eyes red from bawling I left her standing there. They shoved a hose down his throat so I had to hold him.

The Vet stroked his neck, "We need to wash it down his throat. Move it."

"Is he choking?"

"Yes. He ate something he shouldn't have."

"What. I am careful."

Kyle shook his head, "It's my fault. I rode him today, and I left my jacket in the stall. The problem is that I had caramels in my pockets."

I laughed, because I didn't know what else to do, it's a little ironic that being his name. The Vet pulled the hose out and he coughed a couple more times and then shook his head. The vet grabbed a towel and wiped his teeth off, "Well that's enough to scare the shit out of someone."

We all laughed and Sam came storming in, "This is not a laughing matter. He is dead...."

Surprised to see him standing her face grew to a huge smile as she walked around to see his face. Running her hand up and down his nose she asked, "What is wrong with him?"

Kyle felt horrible, "It's my caramels. He got in my pocket and ate all of them."

21 Dancing

Not being able to hold it against her, the way she reacted, I headed up to the tent and check things out. The music is loud as I made my way across the lawn. Not wanting to interfere if there were any young boys that like her or that paid attention to her. It hard for me to allow her to make another mistake, but with our age difference it would be wrong for me to claim her as my own. So protecting her from a far is much better than anything else I can come up with. Plus with how *emotional* she got earlier I didn't want her making any rash decisions to get back at me.

When I walked in I got blasted with the loud music. My eyes took time to adjust to the dim lights. They had strung white Christmas lights throughout the tent giving it a romantic atmosphere. All the girls loved to dance, but the boys all sat at tables off to the side. Well at least I didn't have to witness any of them putting their hands on my Samantha. Shit! Not mine! After finding Sam on the dance floor I scanned the tent for Kyle and Raquel. Making my way to the semi bar I pulled up a seat next to Raquel. I called it a semi because they were serving soda, juice, and waters. Kyle stood behind the bar and asked me if I wanted a soda. I shook my head and glanced out searching for Sam and that scowl of hers wondering if she's still angry. It didn't seem like it because she's dancing and laughing with her friends. Laughing I gestured out to the tables, "What's up with that."

Kyle chuckled, "Too cool."

I remembered when I went to dances, us guys danced too. What is their problem? Tons of girls dancing and they all sat there like lumps on logs.

I leaned to Raquel, "Is she still emotional?"

"No, she is over it."

I raised my eyebrows, "Good. I don't understand how you deal with having two girls."

She laughed.

Tracy walked in with a few of her friends; guys and girls, and they all went out to dance too.

"I didn't have a problem dancing in high school. I had a problem when it ended."

Raquel stood up, "Good, you can dance with me."

Worried that Kyle wouldn't approve I glanced over. He laughed and shooed me to the floor as he shouted out after us, "I'm the guy that is too cool for that."

I laughed as I followed her out to the dance floor. For an older lady she sure can dance. I moved around her and she shook her thing. When my eyes met Sam she glared at me disapproving. She will not scold me while I am having fun dancing with her mother. Taking her hand in mine I spun her and then let her go back out.

She giggles, "A little Fred Astaire?"

We danced till the song was over and then I gave her a hug, "Thank you. I haven't done that in a long time."

Sam came running over, "My turn."

As a slow song came on I took her right in mine while wrapping the other around her waist, "Sam, what are you doing?"

Raising her eyebrows with question she confirmed, "Dancing with you."

So this girl is the one I am in love with? My life will be crazy with emotional ups and downs.

She scolded me, "Kam, I am supposed to put my hands around your neck."

"I don't think so."

She glared at me.

"So, you didn't like my gift?"

"I'm not sure if I should be mad at you or hurt."

"Why. It's the best..."

"That is exactly why. I told you what I wanted for my birthday."

I leaned down and whispered in her ear, "You understand I can't do that."

She pushed me away, "That is why I am mad. When I saw the saddle, it told me I wouldn't get the gift I wanted and that hurt."

"Oh, sorry, but I tried to tell you. We can't go there. You look amazing."

She smiled, "You think so?"

Her eyes sparkled with all the tiny lights when I replied, "Yes."

"Do I seem like an adult?"

Still with the pressure, it's obvious where she's going with this. I rolled my eyes, "Yes."

"Do I act like an adult?"

Not always but I would not tell her that on her birthday, "Most of the time."

She glared, "Do I talk like an adult?"

I sighed regretting my answer before I even said it, "Yes, what is your point?"

She pulled me in further to the front by the DJ. She grinned, "Kam..."

"What?"

She traced her fingers along my waist a little moving closer, "Dose my body represent a woman's body?"

I closed my eyes. She didn't understand that my skin burned where her hand touched me. I squeezed her other hand and opened my eyes to look into hers, "Please, don't make this hard for me."

She gave me that smirk of a little smile, "Okay, now is not a good time, but Kam, I still want the birthday gift I asked you for."

"So, you want me to send the saddle back?"

She shook her head, "They're expensive and you shouldn't have."

"Samantha, you are so special and I thought that would show you how I feel."

"You could show me a different way."

Too much I laughed and kissed her forehead, but I let her go. Making my way back to her parents the only thing that ran through my mind is that Samantha pushed my buttons and now that I shared how I felt she will torture me with it. Today I had my limit and needed to get out of there.

Kyle asked, "So, still moody?"

"Yes. I am calling it a night unless you want help."

"We'll need help in the morning."
"You got it. Good night."

Not sleeping, but day dreaming to drift off when the knocking came from the door. It's not morning yet, so I got up wondering if Kyle needed help with the teens. Walking out I opened my door, but found Sam standing there. Glancing up at the house wondering if anyone noticed her come down here, not sure of what I wanted. If they didn't see her come down she may get that kiss, but if they did... Either way I needed to be strong and direct with her on the subject. I will not give her the birthday kiss she wants.

Sam didn't wait for me to invite her in she shoved her way into the shack. Determined to end this I shook my head, "Sam, I meant it. No and don't make this harder on me."

"I want you to tell me another story about one picture."

"You've heard all my stories, Sam."

"No, I haven't." She walked over and picked up a picture, "This one with you and a little girl holding a fish. Not this one."

She sat down on the love seat and I walked over taking the picture in my hands.

"This is my first girlfriend." I laughed after I said it.

"Why do you laugh and don't you think you were a little young for that?"

"Yes, I was."

"Then how come you had a girlfriend?"

"Because she told me she was."

Sam furrowed her brow with a question.

As I went into the story the memory flashed into my head so vividly.

22 The Fish

I went into the story of how she lived only a few houses down and she showed up every day in the summer. She had been the most stubborn and bossy girl I had met in my life.

One day my dad and I were going fishing. As we loaded the boat with a cooler, the fishing poles, and tackle box Suzie showed up. She followed as I walked into the garage searching for the life jackets. I wanted her to go away so my dad wouldn't ask her to come with, but he couldn't leave her behind. He tried to convince me that she's adorable with that blonde hair, her blue eyes, and those dimples in her cheeks.

He didn't have to deal with her at the playground where she wouldn't let me do anything with anyone else. I had to push her on the swing, hold her hand, and worst of all she made me play house with her. My dad used it as a learning experience telling me this is what I could look forward to when I grow up. Never wanting to grow up because of Suzie, I hated the thought of having to do what she tells me for the rest of my life.

Dad won the argument and Suzie came with us. He finally got to see what I told him about her. The biggest fish hit my line. My pole bent hard I pulled back as dad reached over and pulled up on it with me. We pulled and tugged, but when the fish got near the boat Suzie grabbed my pole pushing me out of the way.

I had to share the rights of catching that fish I was more determined to never share anything with her again. The next day at the playground I yelled at her that I didn't want a girlfriend and I didn't want to play house with her. I wanted to be a boy and shoot some hoops, or play soccer with my buddies. There won't be any more holding hands.

Horse Play

23 Touch

Sam gave me a patronizing gape, "I get your point. You pushed her away because she's too pushy."

"No, I didn't like her."

"You don't like someone who knows what they want. I get it." She got up and almost ran to the door.

Following her to the door I pressed my hand against it holding it shut and keeping her from getting away from me. I didn't want her to torture me, but I also didn't want to hurt her. Our eyes stayed locked while I contemplated what to do.

Her eyes filled with tears, "You don't want me here. I will go."

It's not that I don't want her here because I do. There is nothing in the world that I want more than to have her here with me and to press my lips against hers. Running my fingers through her hair I brought it to my nose so I can take in her scent. She has the sweetest most mouthwatering scent I had ever encountered. Trying to hush her I said, "Sam, it's just not right."

She turned to me, "I'm sorry."

I found myself leaning over her with my head down tracing my face along hers. Pressing her face back into mine we caressed each other as her lips moved closer to mine. I traced my lips against hers and it shot pains of guilt through me all the way to my heart. This is so wrong and I shouldn't feel this way but with her my love runs deeper than anything I have ever experienced. I lowered my hand and placed it on her cheek with my fingers in her hair and I moved to press my lips against hers. *Please make her stop me.* Her mouth moved to mine, and that's when I couldn't stop myself even though I wanted to. I traced her lips with my tongue but only to wrap my lips around hers. Her mouth opened and moved to mine more. I moved my other hand to hold her face to mine. My body tense from the pleasure of kissing her. We both kissed harder and deeper while her hands explored my body moving under my T-shirt igniting my skin.

Making everything okay she reassured me, "I snuck out; they don't know I'm here."

Sucking in a gasp of air I whispered to her, "You shouldn't be here."

Her lips moved to mine again, and I kissed her like I had dreamt about so many times. Pressing my lips around hers to lick and sucked the full flavor of her. My skin warmed under her hands as they worked upward pulling my shirt up as she moved forward. If she didn't stop her touch would drive me insane enough to take her to my room. Having no choice I have to put a stop to this. I let go of her face grabbing her hands and pulled them from me, "Sam, I can't."

She bit her lip and gave me a guilty grin with lips covered in my kisses. Her words broke the silence, "I got my birthday wish. Thank you."

Panting with need and the way she looked me up and down. Heat rushed to the surface of my body to meet her hungry eyes.

Tenderness filled her eyes as she tried to make this okay for me, "The way you touch everything, Kam; the animals, the dishes, and even me when training." She moved up in front of me caressing my cheek with her hand, "Someday when its right for you I have faith that you will be careful with me. I love you Kamron." Her soft lips pressed a light kiss to my cheek before she open the door and slid out the small gap.

As soon as she made it out the door I slid to the floor putting my head in my hands. *What the hell did I just do?*

I went to bed without success of sleeping again. Every time I closed my eyes she stood in front of me begging me to give into the desires. Her scent, her sweetness floated through the air and then I'd had the sensation that her warm moist lips pressed to mine. The worst of it my skin burned with need where her fingers had traced up my back. The temptation too much for me I wanted her to understand that no matter how we see ourselves it's wrong right now. There is too much between us that made it impossible for anything good to come from this.

24 The Pony

Watching for Samantha's bus to arrive anxiously, I wanted to be the one to tell her that we got the stallion in and we're going to breed Daisy. I scrambled to do things quickly so that I could go out and wait for her, knowing that she's going to love this.

I finally gave up and got on the horse to meet her at the end of the drive way. It had to be that time of the day and me full of excitement to be the one to teller her I rushed down the drive. Looking forward to the biggest hug from her, as innocent as it's going to be, it's something that I always welcomed.

I got down when the bus turned the corner coming towards me. The feeling this little girl brings out in me surprises me every time. I couldn't tell you if it's the sparkle in her eyes or the smile on her face that I looked forward to the most. The one thought that I didn't welcome is her getting off the bus holding hands with a young boy.

She didn't even notice me standing here waiting for her. Watching her turn to him and walk backwards with all her attention on him, and he seemed to hang on every word that came out of her mouth. Of course he is in awe over my Samantha. At 15 she is adorable, but she is my...

No she isn't my anything. This is good for her, but it hurt more than I wanted it to. Avoiding them I walkout out to the mailbox keeping the horse between me and her; hoping that I'd avoid contact with her. I'm crushed that she gave this kid all her attention.

Holding back I observed them the whole walk down the drive to the house. If she kisses him in from of me I will make sure they are aware it is in front of me, and if the little bugger gets fresh with my Sam I'll put a stop to it. And here I was looking forward to seeing her eyes bright full of delight and her smile as big as the sunshine, but it's supposed to be for me not for this little punk.

Being in the worst mood I have ever been in my night is shot. Heading back to work I tried to tell myself that I needed to keep to myself and let her live her life.

"Kam... KAM... KAM!!!"
She is not going to come to me and expect me to be excited that she finally made time to find me. I am not answering her.
"Kamron?"
No, don't do it. I need to keep telling myself to not answer her.
"Kamron? Where are you? Kam... Please?"
Shit, "In here." Yeah, I lasted a long time holding a grudge.
She came around the door, but stopped when her eyes fell on me. My heart took off on its own beating wildly, but I stayed natural. The silence almost too much, but those eyes sparkling in a way that told me she knew the stallion is here.
"You didn't come tell me?"
"Tell you what?"
"Boomer! He's here."
I shut the water off and started winding it up, "yep."
"Why didn't you come tell me? I just found out, and I could've been checking him out a long time ago. You knew this is important to me."
"Yep."
"Kam, don't you want to say anything else besides yep?"
"Nope."
"What is wrong with you?"
"Nothing."
"You do realize that this is huge for us?"
"Yep."
"There you go... yep again. Are you mad about this?"
"Nope."

In my head I yelled at her to not come closer to me because she can really hear my thoughts. I need to stay away from her or I will cave.

"KAMRON!"

That caught my attention and my eyes met hers. Again the silence of us caught at the moment waiting for the other to respond. If I said something I may regret it because right now it wouldn't be positive. Forcing myself to have control I finally replied to her pleas, "I tried."

"You tried what?" That came out whiney even for Samantha.

I raised my eyebrows, "I tried to tell you."

She glared at me, "When?"

I shook my head and walked away. I don't have time to argue with her about this. There is work to be done.

She let it go, but followed continuing to explain what she's excited about. "Kam, don't you understand? We are going to have a pony. He is going to have the back end like Boomer, and Daisy's height, Boomer's coloring, and Daisy's spirit. He is going to be the most amazing pony."

I turned just to experience the gleam in her eyes. Her excitement always sparkled in her eyes.

Horse Play

25 Stumble

My birthday came and went before her competition. They didn't make a big deal about it, happy that they didn't. It's a reminder of the reason I do not allow myself to love Sam the way my heart wanted. We worked hard training her and Blaze for the competition. We had a couple more months to get Blaze up to par, but I pushed Samantha as hard as Blaze. This accomplished two things at a time. If she is exhausted from school work and training she wouldn't have time to tempt me into kisses, relieved that it's working so well. She didn't even push for a kiss when we would ride together.

It came to the week before the competition. She's ready, Blaze is ready, and I still had this gut instinct that something isn't right. Like a knot twist and turning my insides with no hope of stopping it. She wanted to work him hard one last time before the competition. Late Wednesday I let her have her way even though I wanted him to have two days rest before the competition. Blaze tripped, caught himself, and pulled out of it, but that's when I sensed the change. The competition is over for them. Blaze won't be able to handle the jumps after that. He'll need time to recover.

I shook my head as she came over trying to make light of it, "He's getting tired. We should call it a night."

Not saying a word I nodded in agreement. She could read my face and my thoughts. She hoped down and followed as I brought him to the grooming area to cool him. Wanting to say I told you so, but couldn't because this hurt her in so many ways.

We cooled him down with the hose and brushing. Without looking at her I sensed her eyes on me. It wasn't until she had made her way stepping in front of me I realized she's trying to change my mind, with her as a distraction. She ran her hand up my arm and linked her fingers with mine as we worked the brush along his back. I leaned forward to take in her scent of fresh air with a hint of her perfume that made her smell like a woman. Her fingers tightened in mine. Her other hand had reached back to my hip pulling me closer. Every inch of my body touched hers; as a man I grew with need. My arms bulged with restraint, my stomach clinched with pain, and my groin grew stiffer. She may try to get me riled up, but she doesn't understand what she's doing to my internal emotions. I had to stop this and her so I whispered in her ear, "Samantha, it will not work."

She turned allowing our bodies to separate. Taking a long slow breath I rested my forehead to hers. Keeping my eyes closed with hopes of not caving because those eyes would win me over if I gazed into them. Her hands slid down from shoulders over my chest as she took a deep breath. We headed for trouble when she unbuttoned the top button of my shirt.

Not allowing it I growled, "Sam."

She didn't stop there. As she undid the next button my breath came a little quicker. This time I asked, "Please..."

But she continued to the third button. Now I have to be firm, "Samantha!"

Leaning forward her breath brushed my skin before her lips grazed my neck.

I gave a breathy exhale of pleading, "Stop..."

Her lips pressed to my chest. They were soft, moist, and determined.

Knowing she's using my weakness to get her way I pulled myself together and grinned, "Samantha, this will not work."

Taking a step back from me she huffed and pushed me away. She made her way around Blaze as my eyes followed her movements. Having to take a few steps to keep her in view she had moved to the front of Blaze working her hands up and down his legs. My heart ached from the pain in her eyes. If she felt it swelling already it's not a good sign for the competition. Six months of training down the tubes because she wanted to use Blaze. There's nothing for me to do to make this better. Standing off to the side I watched as she got out supplies so she could wrap his knee and fetlock. She wrapped ice packs around them and then stood. Avoiding my eyes she spoke, "We should let him rest till Saturday."

Instantly angry that she still planned on riding him in the completion I held my anger as I spoke, "He isn't competing." My eyes stayed fixed on her sure that the tears will come. Her face held no sadness. The only thing that her face reflected was determination as she continued, "We'll wait till Saturday to decide."

Now I yelled, "You can wait all you want, but he's not doing it."

Unlike me, she's more determined to keep her cool as she replied, "Kam, let's just wait until Saturday."

Grabbing her arms forcing her to meet my eyes I firmly explained, "You know he isn't doing this competition."

She gave me the sweetest grin, "I have faith in you and him. It will be fine."

I shook my head not agreeing with her at all.

"I will go. Will you take off..."

That's when her true feelings surfaced. Shit, she will cry if I don't back off. I didn't want her upset, but she had to admit it. He cannot compete.

Holding back the sob she took a deep breath and finished her sentence, "...ice for me."

Not waiting for an answer, she took off at a full run out of the barn toward the house.

"What's that about?"

Why does he have to scare the shit out of me like that? I swear Kyle is just waiting for me to give into Samantha.

Not wanting him to see how much pain his daughter caused me, I went back to work while explaining, "Blazed tripped. There is swelling, and Samantha is upset."

Out of the corner of my eye he stood there observing me, "So that's it?"

How long has he stood there before saying anything? "I tried to let her down without saying I told her so."

"Let her down?"

He is probing for something else. I know he is. If he thinks something is going on with Sam and me then he should just come out and ask. I would tell him the truth. That nothing is going on, or will ever go on for Sam and me. I love her too much, and respect Kyle and his family to let anything happen with or to her. How do I tell him without telling him?

I turned to him determined, "She is not competing. Blaze is hurt. If something happen to her or him I would never forgive myself. She knows I am right, and she didn't want to admit it so she went to sulk by herself."

Why does he grin at me like that? What? He doesn't believe me when I say it's over.

With a chuckle, he replied, "You're sure about *this*?" And he emphasized this, probing for more information.

"Yes!"

"I guess we must take a look at him in the morning."

He turned to walk out but we will not see about anything. I will not let this happen.

"Trust me Kyle. I won't let them get hurt."

I heard him chuckle while walking away, "I will hold you to that."

With his comment my chest eased into a rhythmic pattern as it calmed. He'd back me if he wanted his daughter and horse safe.

26 The Bus

Closing my eyes hoping for sleep, but giving in to thinking about Samantha on the first day I watched her head off to school. At 12 her gumption hadn't settled down since I met her. She stood at the end of the driveway. More like pacing back and forth running her mouth off like she's talking to someone. I chuckled because she carried the conversation on both sides. Holding back my laugh I coughed to make her aware that I approached. When I was her age I had to do this all by myself and I hated that she is out here alone.

"What are *YOU* doing here?"

It didn't sound like she wanted me here. Great! "I thought I'd keep you company."

"I don't need company."

"I can see that."

She glared at me.

"If you don't want me here, I'll…"

She grumbled, "It is fine. If you need to be here stand over there."

Yeah, not going to happen, I will not stand where she tells me to. Did she believe that she could boss whoever she wanted to. Instead I moved to a tree off the road and sat down leaning against it. I took a thick blade of grass and put it between my thumbs. Blowing on it made a whistling sound. She glanced over at me, so I did it again. She made her way towards me. I sat up and crossed my legs as she sat down in front of me the same way. She picked a blade of grass. I showed her how it fit between my thumbs. She did the same. I blew on it and so did she. I chuckled to myself when a smile appeared on her face as she did it again and again. When she stopped blowing on the blade of grass she had a look of inquisitive. I didn't know her question until she asked, "How did you guess I would feel better with you here?"

Warmth filled me as I shrugged my shoulders, "I hated waiting for the bus by myself, so I'm here to keep you company."

She gave me a little smile before she blew on the blade of grass again. This time I watched her as the stress disappeared from her. Her eyes bright, her smile sweet, and she's adorable.

"You look nice today."

She wrinkled her nose and twitched her lip so one side came up with a smirk. Then she bugged her eyes out at me. This little girl made me laugh.

After all her weird faces she asked, "Do you mean nice as in pretty, cute, or nice compared to what I am normally?"

Her sandy blond hair brushed into a soft wave by her face, and the long tangled hair lay neatly in a braid. I took a lock of hair that had come free and rubbed it between my fingers as I looked at her in the eyes, "You are pretty."

She rolled her eyes and shook her head with disbelief. Let off the hook when the bus pulled up she jumped up and ran to pick up her backpack. I did a good job distracting her, and she's not nervous anymore. When she turned glancing back at me I grinned. But she came running back wrapping her arms around my waist, tucking her face to my abdomen, and squeezing, "Thanks Kam. You're the best."

As fast as her hug came it's gone as she got on the school bus. Not wanted to let her go I watched her walk to the back of the bus before she sat down. She'd forget about me now she's on the bus, but her little face appeared in the back window as she waved until I could no longer see her.

From that day forward it would be my responsibility for taking care of her; all the way from being her friend to being her protector.

27 Defiance

Saturday morning came fast enough, but I hadn't thought about the competition at all after Blazes rolled ankle. Sam came down to the barn while I did my chores. Not considering she still planned on competing. She can survey his ankle all she wants, but he isn't doing it.

It became clear she planned to go ahead with it when her dad pulled up with the trailer. Short of losing my temper I stormed towards Kyle, "He is not competing."

"Are you sure about that?"

"Yes. He can't do it."

Sam came running over, "Kam, its better. Come see for yourself. The swelling is better he is fine."

Ignoring here plea I turned to Kyle, "I am telling you no, and I want no part of this because it's unsafe for her and the horse. I can't believe you would let her do this even though I am telling you it's unsafe."

"Kam. Go check his ankle. Then I want your professional decision."

He already has my professional opinion, and he still is asking me to reevaluate the injury. Never in my life have I felt so strong about one thing and this just pisses me off more. After entering the stall and checking out the leg I still felt the same way or maybe even stronger.

Kyle asked, "What do you think?"

"My opinion hasn't changed it will be unsafe for both Sam and Blaze."

Samantha stood there with her fingers in her mouth chewing on them. Not falling for the big eyed innocent daddy's little girl look I glared at her as I demanded that she takes evaluation of this situation, "I thought you understood. He cannot do this without it being dangerous to you or him. You love him so why would you put him in danger?"

She couldn't answer me because she knew I'm right, so she glanced over at her dad with a question on her face.

He fell for her sweetness as he asked me, "Is the swelling down?"

"Yes, but..."

"Is he okay?"

"For now, but..."

"Then I will leave it up to Sam."

I turned to Sam, "You know the answer, Sam. Don't do it."

She took him by the reins and walked out.

As they loaded Blaze into the trailer my stomach turned in knots creating the queasiness that makes you dry heave.

Kyle's eyes met mine, "Are you coming?"

"No, I want none of this. He should not be entered. Why are you letting her decide? I told you it's unsafe for both of them."

He didn't reply before getting in the truck and driving off with Samantha and Blaze. The furry burned inside me until I couldn't contain the anger.

Throwing my truck in park as close to the front gate as I could. My determination to stop her is in full throttle as I ran. Too late to stop her from entering the ring because she had already started so I hand to come up with a new plan as I made my way to the ring. Stopping here by entering the ring would disqualify her and that became my decision.

Barely hearing Kyle, "You showed?" My foot hit the first part of the gate.

He will be angry with me but I will not stop until she does, "Yeah, but something isn't right. This is not right, I sense it."

The first jump small and short, but more determined my foot hit the second board. Kyle grabbed my shirt to hold me back. Second jump over water went well, but neither of them the high jump. My foot lifted to the next board before grabbed my belt holding me back, but if he continues to hold me he's coming with me because I am going over before she gets to the big one. Watching her on the pole jump it's a little higher, less strenuous, but still a good landing for Blaze. Could I be wrong about this? My gut instinct tells me no and up to the fourth board I pushed. One more and I'm over but that's when a second person grabbed my waist pulling me back. Using every strength I had I broke free as she entered the high jump. I'm too late to stop her now. I waited watching here every move as they rose higher than I have ever seen. Blaze in all his glory, and Sam stronger than I have ever seen pride filled me for a split second because that is all I got before they descended.

It's like slow motion when you're watching something tragic happen in front of you. She had given him the freedom to fly, which he did. That isn't the problem; it's the landing that is a problem for Blaze and her. My feet swung over the top of the gate as I watched his front hoof touch down. Every ounce of me hopes I'm wrong and if something will happen it will be when he touches… SHIT! The second his hoof touched down it buckled beneath him and rolled. I made it to the ground before Sam did. Running as if I could catch her in the air and keep her from getting hurt, but the momentum through her over Blaze's head, and my feet wouldn't move any faster. I watched as Sam close her eyes the pain written on her face before even hitting the ground. It's bad enough to see it happening and not being able to do anything, but to watch as her body flips in the air, bounces once and flips her again it tore my heart out to watch as she looked like a rag doll. If Blaze lands on her she'll be crushed. Thankfully his body veered to the right, because of the injured leg, while Samantha when flying straight ahead. I ran to her first hovering over her, "Sam, Sam, open your eyes."

Her eyes found mine but panic filled them as she coughed and gasped for air.

"Shh, don't talk. Just lay here. I'm right here." I wanted to pick her up and cradle her against me, but moving her isn't something you should do.

Her eyes glossed over with tears of sadness because this will not end well. She got out what she wanted to say, "You came?"

"Yes, yes. Now shut up. Don't talk just… it's okay. Don't move the ambulance is on its way."

She coughed out, "Blaze."

"I don't know. You come first. I'm not leaving you to check on him until the medics help you. Where does it hurt?"

"All… breath…" She squeezed her eyes together as the paramedics came to her pushing me away.

That's when I made my way to Blaze who also gasped for air. Holding him down I didn't want him to have more pain by trying to get up, "You're amazing buddy." I stroked his neck, "Stay, calm. I am here. Shh."

I heard Kyle, "Kam…"

So many things to be upset about that the tears fell from my eyes. Not sure if it's putting Blaze down, Sam not being able to say good bye, or that we could have avoided this if they'd listened. Nodding in agreement they gave him an injection that would put him to sleep forever. Holding him, stroking his neck I calmed him until his last breath exhaled and no other air entered his lungs.

Letting Blaze go I got to my feet in time to see Samantha getting pushed into the ambulance. Kyle's hand found my shoulder and I couldn't contain my anger any longer. Turning to him I did something I never thought possible. Going at him I chastised him, "You should have listened. None of this would have happened. If I tell you no ever again you will not question me or I will walk."

He nodded but continued to stare at me.

I raised my eyebrows, "Your daughter."

"And Blaze?"

"I will take care of him. Just go."

He ran to the ambulance getting in with her. There's tons of paper work to fill out, and there will be investigation of safety, but it's our own fault for allowing her to ride. Tears fell the whole time I tried to take care of things. They loaded him up to take him away but asked if they could hold off for a short while. I wanted Samantha to have closure by saying goodbye.

After I got everything done with Blaze I headed to the hospital to check on Samantha. I should have been with her the whole time being her protector, but I had to handle the mistake before I could let it go myself. After checking the emergency room I found out she's admitted, but they didn't tell me anything because I'm not family, but people don't understand what family means.

They must have given Kyle a heads up. He met me at the elevator. Searching his eyes for answers he gave me the low down on Sam, "She's got 3 broken ribs, arm and collar bone, and a torn ACL."

No wonder she couldn't breathe. He led me to her room. Raquel and Tammy had beet me here, but I didn't care what they thought of my reaction. All I can think about is her, in this bed, because I didn't stop her from riding today.

Moving closer to her my eyes scanning everything first. She had three things hooked up with an IV, and her arm bandaged, but no cast. A neck collar held here head in one place. Her leg is not covered, but had a brace holding it straight. If I'd been alone I might have cried for her, but tearing up is bad enough in front of the family. Glancing up at the IV bags I held one at a time gesturing for them to tell me what each one is. Not believing the reality of how bad off she is I stood staring at her.

Raquel got up, "We're going down for food. Kam... Kam..."

Pulling my eyes from Samantha I found Raquel's full of pity. Is it pity for me, or for the guilty feelings I am battling?

"Do you want to come down with us?"

I shook my head no as I moved closer to Samantha. My place is here next to her and will be the rest of my life. Life is too short to deny my feelings for Sam, being right or wrong it's how I feel and someday I will marry that girl, so they are just going to accept that I will take care of their baby. I bent over the bed and kissed her cheek.

Her eyes opened, and she gasped for air. She's in pain and it show on her face. She reached for me pleading, "Kam."

Her word came out weak and sore like it hurt her to even say that. I shook my head, "Shh, don't say a thing."

"But..."

"No, Sam, just calm down. I'm not mad I just want you to be okay."

She gasped, "Pain."

"Do you want me to get the nurse?"

She tried to nod, but the tears seeped out the corner of her eyes. I reached for the call button pushing it a million times before the nurse walked in, "She says she is in pain."

"Yes, she is in pain."

"But we have to give her something."

She smiled at me, "And who are you?"

"Just can you help her please?" I would do anything to get her pain to go away.

The nurse is nice enough but the glare she just gave me I thought for sure she'd call security on me. He walked to the other side of the bed, "This little button here gives her a little dose. It is set up so you can push it when she needs it and it won't give her too much." She touched my hand, "You can help her with it."

I pushed the button looking back at Sam, "This okay?"

She tried to choke out, "Yes," but it's dry and weak.

I grabbed a chair and pulled it up taking her hand in mine, "It's my fault Sam I shouldn't have let you..." Tears escaped me this time, but when I searched her face she had already dosed off again.

Raquel and I stayed at the hospital. We took turns staying by her bed side hour after hour. She sleeps most of the time and it drives me crazy. Kyle took the second night staying, but I refused to leave. Kyle didn't have the same policy as Raquel, so I'm not able to be close to her during his time. I'm sure Kyle had his own issued with guilt about letting Samantha ride that day, his might be deeper than my.

Raquel came the third night, and she allowed me to be next to Sam. I held her hands and talked about the pictures trying to give her stories like I use to. Raquel took a turn, and I slept for a little while, but I moved back in as soon as she would let me. I went back to telling her the stories. I told her about the little girl with the fish again, but it's because I didn't want her to think I didn't love her. This little girl was mean, not like Sam at all. Sam is bossy, but she respects me most of the time.

Raquel asked, "Is this what you do when she goes down to your shack?"

I glanced up, "Yeah, she likes when I tell her about my life and my pictures. She usually laughs at me."

"That's nice that you share your life with her."

I shrugged my shoulders, "She makes me laugh. Her facial expressions; I swear she has a million."

"I do not."

Raquel came over to the other side of the bed as we both stood there staring down at her.

I whispered, "You do, Sam."

"No, you tell good stories."

I laughed and her mother leaned down to kiss her. Samantha has wakened!

28 The Jealousy

Samantha is coming home tomorrow and I can't believe they talked me into coming home and getting a good night sleep before she gets here. This is the first night I've been away from her since the accident. Reflecting on the past year and how much things change remembering how this whole thing started with her dropping the *"I'm Late"* bomb. My mind wandered to that first day Sam and Jared met and how jealous I became.

Samantha happened to be practicing in the ring with me directing her and Jared sat on top of the fence watching the two of us, more specifically her. Sam didn't want to pay attention to me, or listen to direction. All she wanted to do is show off for her audience.

Scolding her for the umpteenth time my voice rose, "Samantha! You need to use your leg muscles."

"I know, Kam."

"Use the reins with your leg movements; you do know how to do this so do it!"

"I know, Kam."

"Hold up." I'm going to get to the bottom of this. "What are you doing?"

With the sweetest grin she asked, "What do you mean?"

I wanted to shake sense into her, "You know how to ride and you can't even direct him around the ring. What are you doing?"

She huffed at me, "Forget it."

Forget what, the training? I will not forget that we are training and if she thinks she can blow me off like... Before I protest any of my thoughts she jumped down, handed me the reins, and headed over to where Jared sat on the fence. Stupid teenagers!

Samantha worked her way up the fence so I got on Baxter to prove a point. Starting with the fundamentals we walked, trotted, and galloped. He did just fine, so the issue was Sam. When my attention moved to her to explain that Baxter is listening just fine I watched her put her hand on Jared's knee and then laugh, to top it off its one of those goofy girly laughs. I've never seen Samantha act like this before. Making my way around the ring again I passed them telling Samantha, "See, just like this."

Ignoring me she moved closer to Jared with a huge grin on her face, "I know Kam."

She's not even paying attention to me or what I am doing. Why do I take time to train her if she's not going to pay attention? "Samantha! You use the reins and your leg muscles like this and he responds fine."

When I turned back to make sure she's paying attention, but my jaw hit the ground while she walked away with Jared. That's it. I've had enough! "Samantha! What are you doing? You're supposed to be training."

She finally gave me her full attention heated with anger, "I know Kam." Then she got a silly grin on her face when she turned back to Jared waving at me, "We're going to go swimming."

She's blowing me and her training off. Why would she act this way? I didn't appreciate how she ignored me in the ring. I got down and brought Baxter in to give him a good rub down. She put her hand on his knee. What is that about? Did she need to touch him like that? I think not! Maybe I shouldn't leave them alone.

The next time I found them together they happened to be walking down the long driveway talking. If I didn't feel like Samantha's protector I'd admit that they seemed like a couple, but that's not going to happen with me around. Samantha is too young for a boyfriend. Getting on Baxter I headed down the driveway quickly after them. Not only are they talking, but they are laughing too. To make things even worse their closeness irritated me.

When I decided I'd had enough that's when Sam bent over picking a piece of grass. She turned to him and… she tickled him with it. They are flirting! Not on my watch!

I rode up quickly, "Samantha, you've got riding lessons in 15 minutes. You need to go get changed because I am not letting you slack on your commitments. As for you boy you got chores that need to get done!"

That anger bubbles deep within me and my ego took over treating them both like children, but that's the problem… They both are.

Horse Play

29 Troubles

Getting her home is one thing but getting her in the house without causing her pain is another issue. Standing back giving her family room to help her is the hardest thing for me. Why they don't just let me lift her into my arms and carry her I have no clue.

First they lifted her legs and turned her so she faced outward, then her dad took her arm to lift her. Here is the tricky part, her ribs are broken on the right side along with her arm, her collar bone is broken on the left side, and the torn ACL is on the right side, so she's not able to support her weight enough to lift herself from a sitting position. Raquel had tears in her eyes as she stood by powerless. Me, I couldn't handle this at all I went down the steps, up the steps to the door, back down to see if I could help, then back up the steps.

When they talked about having Raquel push her out so Kyle could lift her I headed back down the steps. They will hurt her getting her into the house. "Okay, let's not push her out of the car." Squatting in front of her I eased her into my lap and when I got a good hold of her without pressing in the wrong spots I lifted her.

Her dad stood in front of me to take her, but Sam refused. Afraid of being moved again might hurt more. My guess is she likes me holding her, which I didn't mind. She will be my wife someday, not soon, but she will be mine.

After getting her into bed in her room I stood back watching the fuss over her with getting her comfortable and set up for a long stay in her room. After all the disturbance of getting settled in her room she fought to keep her eyes open.

They all kissed her and then headed to the door. Raquel glanced back at me, but I had no plans on leaving. Leaning against the wall, I lowered myself to the floor, "I'll take the first watch."

Her eyebrows scrunched together with distrust, but the slight grin on her face told me she'd let me do this, but perhaps it'll be one time.

Sam's voice came out as a whisper, "Kam, are you still here?"

My eyes stayed on Raquel, "Yes, Samantha. I am staying." To my relief Raquel nodded and let me be. Sam said nothing. With all the silence I drove myself crazy with guilt. It's funny how guilt has a way of making you feel even worse about something you have no control over like here accident.

Her first night home went a little ruff. She woke up every two hours uncomfortable and sore. I helped her roll from one side to the other, then propped up a little, and back to her sides one after the other. By morning I was beat but I still couldn't get myself to leave her side. Hoping to get a cup of coffee I headed to the kitchen. Starting the coffee I rinsed out Sam's water bottle and refilled it.

"So how did it go?"

Jumping out of my skin I turned, "A little rough. She's still in a lot of pain."

Raquel had concern written all over her face, "Do I need to bring something up to her?"

Hoping she didn't plan on kicking me out, "If you want to make her breakfast she could try to eat, and I will take this to her right away."

"That is a great idea."

Relieved I poured her and myself a cup of coffee and grabbed the water bottle heading up to her room.

When Raquel walked in I handed 2 pain killers and the bottle of water.

"How often are you feeding her those?"

"Only what it says, every four hours, but by the third hour she moaned with the pain."

"I'll call the doctor after she's done eating."

I found my spot on the floor by the wall. Afraid to leave this room for long with the idea they may not let me return, but the part they don't understand is that I don't think I'd recover if I lost Samantha. I'm staying right here where I can help her until she's all better.

"Kam?"

Pulled from the cat nap I took I answered, "Right here. You need something?"

"No. You're here."

That seemed to be the question every time she woke. She'd say my name and after hearing my voice back out she went. Sometimes I move to her side to see if she needs a sip of water or another pain killer, but by the time I get there she is back out. My fingers itch to touch her little face, but for now it's not right and I won't give in to my desires. She will be mine soon enough and then I will never let her go, but until then her innocence is precious.

"Kam?"

So faint did I hear her or is that my imagination? I got to my feet and stretched while moving closer.

"KAM?"

Glancing down her eyes still closed I watched her eyes scrunch in distress. Patting her arm, "Sam honey, wake up. You're dreaming."

Her eyes popped open filled with tears and fear.

"What's wrong?"

"You're here?"

"I am. Where else would I go?"

She grimaced as she reached for me. Moving closer I sat on the floor next to her bed taking her hand in mine, "I'm right here. Don't you worry yourself about me leaving because I am staying with you until you can come down to see me on your own?"

That must have been enough because she didn't reply. I made myself comfortable leaning against the side of her bed with her hand in mind. Just when I closed my eyes she said the most amazing thing, "I love you, Kam."

Not wanting to say, yet wanting to confess my deepest truest feelings for her I replied, "I love you too, Sam."

Thinking 'what the hell am I doing' I glanced up to see Raquel standing in the doorway over hearing our exchange. Not sure if she got the whole meaning but the worried look on her face told me she understood. This is more than just a hired hand loving their daughter as a family member. This love is deeper than I could even elaborate.

After the first week Sam would sleep a little longer. It gave me time to slip out early after her first dose of pain killers and back before she needed anymore. In fact I didn't want them to kick me out, so I went to feed the animals before anyone woke up in the house.

Her third week home was the turning point. Now she's awake most of the time, and the painkillers are spaced out even further. We played card games, word games, and I even brought my TV to her room so we could watch TV. As she got better I knew my time with her would end soon. Her dad didn't like me camped out on the floor in her room, but they needed to understand that when they gave me the responsibility to make sure she's safe, even though they let her ride that day, it all comes back on me and my guilt. This is my way of working through it.

My suspicions came true at the end of the forth week. Kyle walked in the bedroom, "I hired someone to help with the chores."

Not wanting to wake Sam I got up while hushing him, "Shh, sleeping." I pushed him out the door. Once in the hallway I asked, "Why did you do that? She is getting better, it won't be much longer."

He grinned, "I need you to get a list done so I can show him what I want him to do. Can you do that?"

"No, I will do them. You should have just told me that the work needs to be done."

He put his hands on my shoulders, "Samantha's injuries are not your fault, Kam. We understand that you feel you need to be here, so he's here to help you. You're still in charge, the horses are yours, but... we still need things done around here, so I got you help."

He didn't kick me out, so I agreed to head down and get him settled in and set him up with a list of work to do. Kyle introduced us. He isn't much older than I was when I first got here. My shack has two rooms, so he's bunking with me, which gives me a better chance at keeping an eye on him. He's not as tall as me at 6'1", he had brown sandy hair he wore messy, and the face of a playboy. Not wanting a player in the same house as the girls my blood heated in my veins.

Giving him instructions I started him on cleaning the stalls which have been neglected for a few weeks now. After getting him everything he needed and showing him where to dispose of the waist I hesitated wanting to give him the speech now, but decided I can do that when I come back to check on him.

"Aren't you the hired help around here? Shouldn't you be helping me?"

"Nope, I've got a sick one I'm helping with."

"In the main house?"

"Yes, the youngest daughter. The girls are off limits. If I find you with either of them I will kill you myself."

Not at all interested he went to work on the stalls. Chuckling all the way to the houses I sobered when I saw Samantha at the dining room table. Taking the seat across from her I asked, "What are you doing?"

"I needed to get out of bed. My body hurts from lying there all the time. Can I ride today?"

"No." Came from my mouth at the same time it came from Kyle and Raquel's. She's good at pushing buttons but we're not going to let her ride before she is healed.

The whole day she spent trying to argue with me that the best thing for her would to be to ride as soon as possible. I'm not falling for any of her reasons, or pleas.

I went down to the barn to check on Adam and bring him back to the house for dinner. He didn't even finish the stales. Samantha could have finished it faster even in her beat up body. Not complaining I dug in and helped with the rest of the stalls. Any help is better for me because it made it okay for me to be at the house with Samantha.

The dinner table set they gave him the chair next to mine and across from Tammy. The way she stared at him and the glances he took at her it will be a challenge to keep them apart. Wanting to forewarn Kyle about the way they gaze at each other torn with being okay with it as long as it's not Samantha. Nothing will happen in the next few days with me keeping him busy trying to get everything caught up in the barn and fields.

Sam didn't pay him much attention, but Tammy did. She was asking a ton of questions but pleased when her dad scolded her, "If he has to keep talking he won't be able to eat. Hush now girl, he worked hard today and needs food."

Adam was enjoying the attention, so I knew I would have to warn him again.

Heading out the door to walk him down to the shack Sam stopped me, "Kam, we are having family movie night. Will you come back and watch movies with us?"

I'd never say no to her when I can spend more time with her, but I looked at Kyle and Raquel for approval. They both encouraged it so I said yes.

"Wear your pajama's. It's tradition."

I laughed as I walked out. I don't have pajamas.

30 The Pajamas

Trying to think of what I will wear for pajamas I walked in looking at the pictures for inspiration. Wondering what I had worn every time she had come down. It has been so many times now it's hard to remember. Jeans, sweats occasionally, but shorts?

Seeing her pick up the picture of my father and me as a smile grew over her face, "Is this your dad?"

"Yes."

"You look like him."

I walked over taking the photo in my hands to remember him. He is one of the real reasons I left. Maybe I'm more like him than I want to admit.

"You never talk about him Kam."

I shook my head. We had argued to the point of him kicking me out, and me saying I would never go back. "We got in an argument."

She asked no questions, but she took the picture back and sat down on the couch staring at it. I moved to sit by her. It amazed me that with how much her mouth ran, she sat silent this time. Is she waiting for me to tell her something? Wanting to blame him my mind screamed, *he's a stubborn old man*, but I spoke the truth, "I was young and stupid." Saying the stupid part because it's my fault we fought.

"So what happened?"

For being so out spoke, so honestly pure, she is also caring.

I spilled my guts to her explaining that it was a stupid argument. My dad was showing a horse, so when the customer asked a question that compared us to the Livingston's down the road I felt betrayed. I said the wrong thing, which made dad glare at me. It's not like I bad mouth the Livingston's but they were useless and their horses didn't have the training ours did. My dad sent me away until he wrapped up with the customers. I didn't get why we would let them wager a lower price for the work we'd provide when they could get it a lot cheaper with the competition. When my father found me I got a lecture of a lifetime. The hard part is the demeaning nature they were treating him, and I told them off. We argued more, my determination to make him see he's worth caused him to grow even more infuriated. The harder I tried to tell him that he is much better than that, the more he insisted that he didn't have to do business that way, because his work spoke stronger than any words. The argument got heated so when I got in his face arguing my point he hit me. It wasn't the shock of the blow that put me on the ground. He had never hit me like that before and he'd never do it again and I left. After I left it dawned on me that he wouldn't have ever hit me if I didn't push him into. When I glanced back at Samantha I saw she felt my pain. Not the pain he caused but the pain in my heart for hurting my father twice that night. Not being able to go back is even more painful. When I stopped pacing I sat back down next to her.

She grabbed at my paints, "Where are these from?"

The pants I wore are my fathers from when I came into the world. When I left I took them thinking he didn't have the right to be my father if he hit me like that. They're hospital pants.

As I changed into them for the pajama party I wondered if Samantha would remember the story.

31 Movies

The night went fine. I started by sitting on the other end of the couch from her. I helped Raquel make popcorn. Sam lounged with her feet on me which I rubbed. I got up to help Kyle with the Ice cream and then sat on the floor in front of Sam to eat my bowl. We sat through three movies before Kyle and Raquel retired to bed. I got up to leave but Sam begged, "Just one more please?"

I shouldn't stay if her mom and dad were going to bed. She's doing better, and she might tempt me into kissing her. Kyle stopped and looked at me with questioning eyes, "It's okay, Kam, if you want you can stay for one more, but can you help her upstairs if she needs it?"

Torn between staying and spending time with her, but I also didn't want to give her the opportunity to lure me in. With her being in a compromising way I wouldn't be able to say no. Not able to express my internal battle I nodded and sat back down. She nuzzled into the couch again pulling covers up around her, "I remember what you told me the last time you wore those, it made me sad?"

"I wondered if you'd remember."

Running her fingers through my hair she replied, "I do remember. Have you contacted him?"

"No."

Her fingers lingered at the back of my neck where the goose bumps were growing. "Then why did you wear those? Are you trying to torture yourself?"

Leaning my head forward her fingers kneaded my neck. Though I enjoyed it I turned to her making her stop the massage, "I don't have pajamas."

"You don't have pajamas?"

"No."

"Why not?"

"I don't know. I guess I don't need them."

"What do you sleep in then?"

Was this a trick question, "Boxers."

"Oh."

I waited for something else from her, but she didn't go further with the subject so I didn't say anything.

She didn't make it through the movie. Her breathing grew heavy, so I glanced back finding her out cold so I decided now would be good as any time to get her up stairs. I got up picking her up with me. She grimaced, "Oh, Kam, no you can't carry me."

Easing her back down I asked, "Does it hurt?"

"Yes."

Waiting for her to tell me how I should help her. She grinned slightly, "This is what I deserve for not listening to you."

"No, don't say that. You don't mean that."

"Yes, I do. You tried to tell me, but I didn't want to hear it. I don't want you to think I don't listen to you because I do every word of it. In fact I think you are the only person I hear."

Pain ripped at my insides as I thought about Blaze, "I asked them to hold off on taking care of Blaze. After finding out how long your recovery could take I had to let them go ahead with the procedures. You didn't get to say goodbye and I am deeply sorry about that."

"So am I. It was my fault."

"Things happen, Sam. I am just glad we still have you."

She smiled slightly and gave me her hand. Pulling her to her feet I wrapped my arm carefully around her to give her support. My whole body tensed as she leaned her forehead to my chest running her hand down it. I closed my eyes feeling the rush of blood to my skin where she touched. With a whisper I encouraged her to get moving, "I have to get you up stairs so I can go."

"Kam... when will you kiss me again?"

That's an easy one, a long time from now, "When you are my age."

"I will never be your age because you will continue to get older too."

Shit, she caught that. Teasing her so I don't have to give her the truth may not work for long. I shook my head, "You are a funny girl. Upstairs."

She turned from me, but I took her good arm and wrapped it around me as we made our way up the steps one at a time. Once tucked into her bed I leaned over her to kiss her forehead, "Sweet dreams."

Even though I didn't give her a straight answer she didn't push for one. In fact she fell asleep as soon as her eye closed. My sweet little Samantha is growing into a beauty before my eyes and being this close and not kiss her is going to be more difficult with each day. Thankful that today went that well, and that she did not push me.

Horse Play

32 The Words

Falling to my bed relieved that the night had gone so smooth but knowing the rest of my night will not be so kind. Her asking for a kiss brought back the memory of the first time I'd seen her as a hormonal teenager. My day had been long and hard when I caught her watching me instead of working hard with me. I was irritated with her until her eyes met mine filled with want.

Kyle walked into the Stall, "How is the addition coming along?"

"Good. I came to feed the horses, but I left Sam setting up the water lines and the feed buckets."

The smile on his face grew with whatever he had going on in his brain. Not sure what the grin was about he moved from the stall. The urge to follow him gnawed at me, but things needed to be done and I still had a fence to finish. The new barn is larger than the old one, with 14 stall on each side, wide open alley, large overhead doors on both ends, and another fenced in area to showcase the horses. This addition will be huge for the family and for me as their trainer.

After getting the rest of the horses fed I headed back to finish working on the fence. Kyle wanted to hire someone I wanted the extra cash, so I offered to do it for a little money to tuck away. Someday I would need a place of my own so making more money doesn't hurt. Taking my time making sure each piece of railing fit snug before securing it. Building the pen myself felt good, accomplished, and proud. Someday I would have a fence to build at my home. I can picture it. The house I'd have, a two story with a porch that wrapped around the house so we could enjoy every view of our property, and a large barn like the new one that Kyle put in. Samantha and I could sit in a swing on the front porch listening to the birds chirping, and the horse neighing in the pasture. We could even lay a blanket in the yard, stay out to see the stars and make love outdoors.

Glancing up to make sure that no one had noticed my day dream about Sam. She is on her way down to the barn with a great big grin on her face, and a sucker stick coming out from her lips. The challenge I face now is avoiding watching her move that sucker in and out of her mouth. I think she does it on purpose to get me to give in to my grueling need for her, or maybe not, either way it has the same effect on me, I will not allow myself to act on this.

Making sure we went top of the line on the rink fencing it was hard heavy wood, making my job challenging. Lifting, hold, and screw the screw in on one side then making the way to the other. Lifting, I would do the same then add 3 more screws for a good support on each post.

"How's it going?" She asked in her little girl voice.

When she talks with her baby talk I almost don't want to talk to her, but talking will not kill me, "You're not dressed to help me?"

"Nope. Guess what?"

"Sam, I don't have time to play guessing games what do you want if you're not here to help me?"

"Forget it."

"What?"

"No big deal. It's just dad has Toronto on his way. I wanted to make sure this will be ready."

"When will he arrive?"

"Tomorrow around noon,"

"I think it will be ready if I could get a little help from you."

"Nice try Kam, but I'm supposed to go to town with mom."

"Then get. You're distracting me."

The fence is a new design and we are going a little over board, but it will be steady, and strong. A post every 8 feet and 5 cross ways. The top has a ledge large enough for sitting on, and an open space between the top rail and the next one down for viewing. Feeling proud of the design that I came up with; I glanced back to see if Samantha headed back to the house yet, but she still lingered by the gate. She must be worried if I'll have it done by tomorrow. "Sam, you have nothing to worry about. I'll get it done."

Steady focus, determination will get me through this last half. All the posts set 4 days ago so the setting has had plenty of time to cure. Each rail going up one by one as I take my time to make sure that every rail is perfect. In reality it took me about 5 min for each rail, so if I kept going I'd have it done by dinner time. It's bothering me she is still sitting there while I'm working, because I would love to glance up at her and see that smile she gives me, but I need to keep my mind on what I am doing. "Thought you were going to town?"

"Yep."

Lifting the next rail with my left arm and screwed it in with my right. This is getting easier and easier as I get used to it. "You could help until you have to leave."

"Nope."

Chuckling to myself, I need to ask why, "What's so important in town that you can't help me until you go?"

"Mom doesn't want me to get disheveled."

This girl put a smile on my face, "So what's so important that you shouldn't get dirty?"

"SAM!"

Glancing up hoping she'd answer me before taking off but the girl sitting on the fence is no girl, but a young woman yes. As my eyes trailed up her I saw the curl on her mouth as my eyes grazed over it until my eyes met hers. Her eyes grew dark like dusk moving in. It's not until she bit her lip did it register that her hormones were going crazy over watching me.

A touch embarrassed by the way she's staring at me I grabbed the towel hanging out of my back pocket and tossed it at her, "Sam, your mom yelled for you."

Startled out of her trance she got down but peaked back through the top rails, "Kam!"

Stopping, I gave her my full attention, "Yeah?"

Her eyes lit up, "I love you."

The only problem with saying I love you, that is more than a kiddy crush and we both felt the pull. She will marry me someday, but until then she needs to experience her life with people her age. Wanting her to understand I stared into her eyes, "I love you too, kiddo."

Her dad walked out of the barn as I got to the "you" part so I added the kiddo for him, but she gets it. Her eyes filled with sparkles as Kyle hurried her, "Your mom's ready. Get going."

We both watched her run all the way to the driveway where her mom waited for her. I went back to work before facing Kyle.

"I like the kiddo part." Kyle referenced my comment to Sam.

What can I say to him, "She's a good kid."

Hoping that would be enough I went back to working on the fence rails.

"KAM!"

Coming to a stop once again I turned to him, "Yeah?"

He hesitated, thinking a little longer about saying what is on his mind, but it's obvious he has something to say. "Um…, it's just… you're a good man, and I wanted to… Ah, hell with it."

Setting everything aside; I grabbed my water bottle took a long swig, and then offered it to him. I understand what he's trying to get out without saying it. He took a long swig of the water and we stood there for a minute. There is no need to tell me to keep my hands off because I would without him saying it. "I understand."

He glanced at me with a crooked grin, chuckled a little, shook his head then walked away, "You are a dam good man Kamron. I'm thankful that it's you here with us."

As he headed back to the house I yelled after him, "So am I! So am I."

33 Challenges

When she went back to school I saw little of her. In fact, I see Tracy more than Samantha. For Tracy it's all about 'Adam'. It irritated me when she pretended to be interested in the horses because it's obvious what she's interested in.

Well, after Christmas Sam came down to spend time with me and the horses. The only problem with that is I'm working with a pair of two-year-olds her dad just took in. They were a handful and the inside arena held a chill. She propped herself up on the gate to watch the session. It wasn't long till she was laughing. I glared at her from a distance, "If you think you could do better get your butt out here."

She jumped down from the fence giving me a heart attack. She is all healed but my instinct to protect her makes me want to put cushions all the way around her blocking anything from hurting her. Hell I don't want to let her on a horse again, but that might be a little extreme so I am coming to terms with my protectiveness.

"So, who are these two?"

I laughed, "Your dad must like John Cougar Mellencamp, because their names are Jack and Diane."

"Who?"

"Old rock-and-roll song, forget it."

"No, now I want to hear it."

I laughed while giving her the reins, "I will play it for you someday."

Glancing over my shoulder to watch her mimicking everything I do with Jack, but with Diane.

She asked, "Easier with two people?"

"Yes. Thank you."

She helped me for about an hour and then we headed in to cool them down. It was cool outside, and we didn't work them hard so we didn't have to do much, just a quick brushing.

There was something that was bothering me about Adam and Samantha's easiness on him so I need to ask her about it. "Sam, you didn't drill Adam like you did me, why not?"

She stated quit clearly, "Because he is not the trainer."

I glared at her, "So, you don't care if he knows anything?"

"Nope."

"Tracy seems to like him."

"Yep."

"I knew it. I will kill him."

She had stopped walking, so I turned to make sure she is okay. I don't want her hurt ever again. The hurt in her eyes is far worse on my heart then a broken bone. Wanting to run my hands over every inch to find where her pain was I moved closer, "What is it?"

"You care that she likes him?"

Finding out it's not a physical pain I tried to explain, "No; yes; more like I have to protect your family."

She still didn't move and her eyes threw spears at me. Her reaction is uncalled for. She has to understand that she's the one for me even if I can't show her how much I love her. Standing here looking at her with that expression on her face makes me weak at the knees. Guys aren't supposed to feel that way anyway, but she could twist me into knots if she wanted to. To support my toughness I headed to the grooming area without her.

She was slow to follow me, but she wandered in. I peeked at her over Jack while I continued to brush him. She didn't come in to help me, but she came to sit on the counter behind me. I tried not to pay attention, but it had been a long time since she spent time with me.

I was hesitant to ask, "So, do you have any pain?"

"Nope, in fact I've thought about this Kam and I will ride today."

Every muscle in my body went ridged and I closing my eyes to contain my anger enough to grit out, "Are you sure you want to do that?"

"Yes, but I will leave it up to you who I can ride."

Relief came over my body as I turned to grin at her, "You will let me pick?"

"Yes, as long as it's not Betsy."

I laughed, "That is exactly who you will be riding."

"You're not funny. She won't move an inch if I am on her."

"I know. It's perfect." I gave her a grin so she couldn't refuse me.

She stuck her nose in the air, "Fine, I'll ask my dad?"

"You do that, you stubborn little thing you."

"Fine I will."

I raised my eyebrows, "Well, go then."

Her expression changed, "You want me to leave?"

"No, I expect you back in 15 minutes to tell me what horse you will ride."

She jumped down and ran yelling for her dad. Satisfied before she asked because he said he would never doubt me again or I'd leave.

Holding my grin back became a challenge when he entered with her. Avoiding the topic of Samantha riding he picked up a brush to help me while she followed him anxiously.

After Samantha coughed as a reminder why he is here he broke the silence, "So, Sam says you'd have her ride Betsy?"

Raising my eyebrows questioning his intentions, "Yes, don't you agree with me it's a good idea?"

As he searched my face hoping to see me break a smile he became disappointed when I did no such thing. Nothing like a rooster fight, we'd never let it get that far. When he gave up his want for questioning me he turned to Samantha with every intention of explaining. I swear that little girl could have anything she wants when he begs with her eyes like that, so her dad didn't even get one word out before he turned back again. He wants to give me an order, he wants to tell me I'm over reacting, and most of all he wants to tell me to pick a different horse. Clearing his throat, "Kam, is it possible you might be a little strict with Samantha?"

My turn to give him my 'ready to fight' glare, "I told you that my decision stands or else... If she wants to ride today it will be Betsy and possibly Clark Bar tomorrow. Depending on how she does we'll work our way up the ladder. Who knows she might even ride Jack here in a year."

Samantha let out a screech, "Dad that is not fair. I should be at least allowed to ride Grey."

He grinned at me, "No. Whatever Kamron says goes. Sorry dear. Deal with it."

He walked out just, so he didn't have to deal with her determination to have her way. Not a peep escaped her lips but her eyes went to slits of evil while she moved closer, "What do you have on my dad that he didn't side with me?"

Backing up step by step until my back was against the counter while she continued to advance until her fist met my shoulder. Not letting her get carried away I moved closer as I gripped her punching fist in my hand, "First, it's not nice to hit me. Second..." I leaned down so that my lips were an inch from her making me want to press them to her firm pressed lips, "My leverage is you."

She stopped struggling, her eyes meeting mine, "What do you mean?"

I grinned and let her hand go moving in closer and closer and then whispered to her lips, "After your accident I told him if he ever went against my wishes again I would leave. Your life is very important to me, so I have strict rules."

Her little hand came to my mouth covering it. She stared into my eyes and I held her hand to my mouth and kissed it. When I opened my eyes she stared at me in the sweetest way. It was like I gave her the best news she's ever heard, "Okay."

Her eyes filled with tears while I grinned, "So, you will ride Betsy if you want to ride today?"

She nodded and backed away taking Jack with her. Heading in the opposite direction I led Diane into the grooming area.

Dealing with Samantha can be *trying* enough but as Adam walked in with a smirk on his face my day is doomed with hard situations.

"You said the girls were off limits?"

This will not be discussed. Glaring to get my point across I scolded, "They are."

"But I saw you with..."

I gave him the '*I will kill you*' look, and he stopped talking. It did little good because he couldn't keep his mouth shut, "Isn't she a little young for you?"

"Yes."

"Then why...?"

I glared at him again. If he kept this up I will kill him.

"Oh..."

The grin on his face told me that this discussion is not over. It will come back to haunt me later. My mind already wandering off to him and Tracy, and me having to keep my mouth shut so he wouldn't bring up my feelings for Samantha to attention. Even if I can't make him keep his distance with my mouth I sure as hell can make him keep his distance with my fist. Wiping the smirk from his face with my fist could be rewarding.

I headed to the arena where Sam had Betsy saddled and bridled. I helped her up and then she gazed down at me, "If it goes well can you please pick a different horse tomorrow?"

If she would have given me those eyes, and that soft plea when I first told her who she could ride I would have caved like I'm about to do now, "Yes, fine."

Horse Play

34 The Lead

The first time she looked up at me with pure innocence it rocked my world. She left me speechless for a long time that afternoon.

Kyle had picked up a wild mustang and Samantha claimed him before I even evaluated him. Kyle advised me I will help Samantha break him. In my opinion she is a spoiled brat that gets whatever she wants. Not really, but Kyle sides with her more times than I can remember him siding with me, especially when the situation could be dangerous. The part I hated the most is when Kyle says he believes in my abilities to train her to train the horse. He doesn't see I have a gift that not everyone has. I don't have to push the horse or grind them or anything else in a negative way because they get met right away. They sense my confidence, my ability, and my easy steady way.

She stood in the middle of the ring with the led waiting for me to direct her on the next step. Taking things slow I had her walk him in a circle using clicking sounds from her mouth and the tug of the rope. Storm is a five year old that has lack of training so he's a little hesitant making me nervous about leaving her in the ring by herself. Sam at 14 could handle it all. Next, I directed her to stop while he slowed, face him, and then switch directions to circle the other way.

After switching back and forth Storm settled down a little, so I had her stop for the next step. Gaining trust and teaching him who's in charge is the next step of our training. I moved into the ring with her teaching her how to hold the lead, how to push him back with a shake of the lead, how to have him walk along with her, how to back up. We spent the first half of the day working him.

For a wild mustang he sure was responsive. Following her lead, allowing her to direct him, but touching is still out.

It was when she made a quick move that startled him he reared. Shoving Samantha behind me I took the hit in the chest first pushing me back into her we lost our footing together as we fell back me landing on her. Storm went wild with neighs, bucking, and wildness. Intent on not letting Samantha get hurt I rushed to my feet, rushed to Storm grabbing for the lead. That was all it took for him to realize that I'm the boss and he settled down instantly while I led him from the ring back to his stall. When I made my way back to the ring she still laid there. I rushed to her hovering over her touching her little legs, arms, and face searching for where she's hurt. We must have fallen clumsily enough that she is hurt.

"Sam, where does it hurt?"

Those eyes wide with fear bore into mine. She is so innocent and pure her drawl made me pull her to my lap, "Sam, please tell me where you're hurt?"

That's when she lost it. It must have scared her because now her shoulders moved up and down while she sobbed in my arms. Tracing my hand along her back trying to calm her I asked, "Are you hurt?"

Relief filled me when she shook her head, she's not hurt. Next question then, "Did that scare you?"

Again she shook her head no. If she's not hurt or scared why is she sobbing in my arms right now? Clearing my throat, I had one more question, "Why are you upset?"

Her fingers played with the front of my shirt while I waited for her to calm down enough to tell me what's gotten to her this way. She is not a soft little girl full of hormones so it has to be something significant.

"Samantha, help me out here. I need to know if we need to get you to the hospital or not." I placed my fingers under her chin lifting her face hoping her eyes will tell me the answer. When her eyes met mine so pure and innocent I stopped breathing. It held there as if I didn't need air to live. I didn't even realize it until she spoke releasing me from my stall.

"Kam, you protected me. You put yourself in harm's way to save me." She wrapped her arms around me tight, "No one has ever put me before them like that. I love you Kam."

"Is everything okay over there you too?"

Kyle headed in our direction. It didn't take but two seconds to lift Samantha to a standing position and pushing myself up beside her.

"Sam is everything okay?"

Kyles eyes went from his daughter to me and back again. As if I made advances toward her. Still stunned by Sam's eyes I couldn't say a word. In my head I tried to sort out the feelings she stirred in me. She glanced back at me while answering her dad, "He saved me from getting kicked in the face; took the blow that Storm intended for me to his chest. Are you okay, Kam?"

Shaking my head intending to rid it of other things that distracted me I smiled at Kyle, "I'm good. It wasn't as amazing as she's making it sound. The truth is, I fell on Sam and thought I hurt her in the fall, so when she cried it freaked me out."

His eyes scrutinized Sam, "You cried?"

That's when Kyle ran his fingers over her hands, arms, and shoulders, "Are you sure you're okay?" He was turning her to the house walking her that direction before she glanced back at me with sorry filled eyes. Chuckling to myself over the protectiveness of her father I gave her a little wave knowing she'd be well taken care of.

35 Best

Spring time is here and Sam is riding like her old self. She's back to her old tricks and a pleasure to watch. Tracy and Adam are sneaking off on a regular basis, and I hated that I had to keep my mouth shut. Sam and I are just that. Sam is herself, and me I'm a lost cause in love with someone I couldn't allow myself to be with, at least not now.

Samantha likes to surprise me sometimes showing up for a story from my past. Today seems to be no different. Allowing her to enter I held the door open wide for her. Making her way to the love seat she sat down keeping her eyes on me. Not sure of the surprise visit I stayed near the door waiting for her explanation.

"Kam, I need to talk to you."

I walked over to stand closer, but not taking a seat. My fear of her tempting me out weighs my need to be by her.

"Kam. Please? I am serious because I need to see what you think about something."

I sat down staring at her reserving my right to be cautious.

"Is Adam here?"

Shit! This will be about us. I should have said yes.

"Kam, I am torn up about something and I want your opinion."

That doesn't sound like this has to do with us so I nodded cautiously. In my head I pleaded, *"Please don't ask me to kiss you."*

"Okay... you see... I'm not sure how to..." She looked up at me torn.

Her actions told me that her intentions are not to tempt me so I relaxed a little. This could be a serious problem and she wants my opinion. That makes me happy.

She scooted closer, facing me, and took my hand in hers. Shit, she will tempt me. God, please give me the strength to say no.

"Um, you agree that we like a lot of the same things?"

While agreeing with her I nodded.

"You understand that I like to be around you more than anyone else?"

Grinning like a fool I nodded again. Complementing me like this she is up to something I will not approve of. She is going in circles on this one.

"Well, I can already guess what you will say, but I need you to say it, because it's not right if I don't ask you first."

"Sam?"

"Prom! You will tell me you can't, but I like spending time with you. We complement each other, we like the same things, you don't give into me, and I just want you to go with me to share my special night. Please Kam tell me you'll go with me?"

She has the saddest puppy dog eyes I had ever seen. How can I tell her no? She wants me to be part of her life outside of here and it breaks my heart I will hurt her, "I can't."

Not wasting any time she got up to leave. I grabbed her hand holding her there not wanting to let her go.

The pain that filled her showed in her voice as she stuttered, "I would rather…"

Finding it hard to explain my answer I asked her, "Who will you go to the prom with?"

"That jerk, Tyler."

Hearing that assholes name it sent sears of pain into my chest like a knife. Closing my eyes to avoid letting her see the red that has to be boiling over I asked, "Why?"

"Because he is the best, and he asked me." Her tone is full of sarcasm.

"What do you mean?"

"He is the Captain of Football, Basketball, and Baseball teams. How can I say no?"

I'm not happy with her choice at all, "Easily!"

"Not so easy. No one will ask because he put the word out he's asking me. So, I don't have a choice."

"Are you going to the party after the dance?"

"Yes. Doesn't everybody?"

"But, he will…"

"Yes, he will. That makes you the better choice."

"Don't Sam."

She traced her hand along my face, "I won't make a mistake again, Kam. I wish you'd go with me."

She walked to the door and stopped for just a second.

"Sam?"

"Yeah."

"I'm sorry."

"So am I."

She left and my heart beat hard against my chest. This is the worst feeling next to watching her in the competition that almost took her from us. What am I going to do now?

Horse Play

36 The Date

This night will be a struggle; my mind wandering to Samantha going to prom with a guy that will make moves on her. No, I can't let my imagination run wild like that. Drifting back to her first date and remembering how much it irritated me that her parents said yes. She was 15 at the time.

I came in for dinner late and it seemed like everyone has something on their minds because it's crazy quiet. Trying not to dwell on it because everyone has full plates and my stomach is growling. As if this is normal everyone handed me dishes of food for me to fill my plate. As soon as I took the first forkful of food it became clear that this will not be a normal dinner.

"Tracy, how old we're you when you went on your first date?"

The lump in my throat stopped me from swallowing as my eyes landed on Samantha. She seems calm, confident, and determined. What is she up to this time?

Regaining my ability to continue I chewed and swallowed waiting to take the next bite. I didn't want to choke on the food if she came up with something I'd hate hearting.

Tracy didn't answer; Raquel spoke instead, "She was 15, but it was a group date."

Something weird is happening between Raquel and Samantha. They both have little smirks on their faces. Taking a glance at Kyle for his recognition, but he didn't seem to notice how off this felt.

"Yeah, mom dropped me, Katie, Ashley, and Rachelle off at the movie theater where we met Scott, Brandon, Michael, and Cory. It's not that bad and Katie's mom picked us up right after the movie was over."

My attention turned to Tracy. This is a plot. Kyle has to see through this. This time my eyes fell on him. If he didn't get what is going on then I'd be letting him in on it. They will not let her date at 15. Can I say this again? She's only 15 years old and if I may say so myself she's still a baby! Kyle should ask me what teenage boys think about because I was once a teenager so I know where their dirty little minds are. It will not happen with my Samantha. Not if I have anything to do with it. I need to stop this from happening, "Wow, that's young isn't it?"

Samantha's eyes rose with a glare as they penetrated into me, "How old were you when you went on your first date."

She will not get that answer, "I'm a guy."

All three of the girls, woman, no, the females at the table glared at me. Raquel interrupted the silence, "And what does that mean?"

Kyle held back a chuckle while I tried to come up with the correct answer, "Um... What I meant is... 15 years old is young, isn't it?"

Raquel set her fork and knife on the table. My eyes focused on her and what she's doing as her hands went beneath the table top. Startled when she asked, "You didn't say what you mean by that?"

With hope of more time I took a huge forkful of food and shoved it in my mouth hold up one finger. How do you explain that 15-year-old boys think about getting into a girl's pants, or playing with their breast, or kissing the girl senseless to get more of what he wants from her? Teenage boys are focused with one brain and that is not the one in their heads. We come to terms with these needs as we get older. I didn't want Samantha exposed to those needs at the age of 15.

Raquel's patience ran thin, "We're waiting Kamron."

Oh, shit she used my full name. Okay here it goes, "It's not that it makes it okay by any means, but teenage boys are more focused on one thing, and it's not that I don't think Samantha can't handle..."

Kyle interrupted, "Okay ladies that is enough. Kam is trying to protect all of you. Raquel, settle down honey. Be glad that Kam remembers what it's like at that age and wants to help keep our girls safety."

Samantha protested, "But he is not our father, or our big brother or anything like that. He shouldn't have a say in what age we can date."

Kyle laughed, but the conversation is taking an uncomfortable turn. I took my silverware and plate making to move away from the table, "If you will excuse me it's none of my..."

"Oh, no you don't." Raquel insisted. "So tell me why Samantha shouldn't go on a group date with a fifteen year old boy."

"MOM!" Samantha blurted out because I spoiled the casual leading up to asking Kyle if she could go.

Tracy busted out laughing, "Well that went smooth."

I sat back down and avoided everyone's eyes. I am happy that I put it out there that she's too young and now it's up to them. They better make the right choice...

It wasn't two weeks later when Samantha went bouncing by me in the barn dressed in straight legged jeans that fit like a glove, and a cute girly top which didn't fit Samantha's regular attire. What the hell is she doing? She leaned into Kyle's office, "Dad, I'm leaving."

Where is she going dressed like that? I ambled towards the office.

"You look adorable, sweetheart."

Yeah she did. The way she's dressed made her appear to be 18 years old. It piqued my interest, "Where are you going?"

She glanced back at me, "Thanks dad. I will see you about 9:30. Bri's mom is picking all of us up. It will take a while to drop everyone off."

"Where are you going?" Why wouldn't she answer me?

"Love you Sweetheart. Have fun."

"Love you too dad." She turned away from the door and now faced me as she continued to talk to her dad, "How fun can a movie be? We will sit still and watching a movie."

No! No! NO! She is not going on a date. She gave me a little grin while walking towards me.

I didn't want her to go, but what could I say? Samantha I want you to wait until you are 18 and fall in love with me; yeah cuz that will happen. It still wouldn't be right, even at 18 for her because I continue to grow older too and I'll be 26.

She stopped in front of me, with her eyes wide and innocent, "Unless you can tell me why I shouldn't go, you should tell me to go have fun."

Lowering my head to give her a private compliment, "You look beautiful Samantha, so just be..."

That put a smile on her face. Not what I wanted either. I wanted her to know that teenage boys are... Oh hell with it. She should be with someone her age. At least they can experience stuff together... No, I can't deal with that thought, "Have fun Samantha."

She giggled, wrapped her hand around my forearm, turning me in the direction she headed, and explained it the way she sees it, "Kam, it's not like a real date. We're going in a group. Three of the guys like Bri, not me."

I stopped, pulling her in front of me, "What do you mean that three of them like Bri? You are the cutest one of all your friends. You act more mature than any of them, and you are smarter about things. Why would any boy be more interested in Bri than you?"

Her eyes softened, as I spoke the truth, but when I got done she grinned, "Kam, do you want me to answer that?"

So confused until she widened her eyes suggesting that I get what she meant. Realizing she had other meaning I asked, "She is a little more experienced with boys?"

Samantha turned to continue walking without denying or confirming. I caught up to her, "Samantha?"

"No, but she wants to be I guess. She wants the boyfriend, and I want to be friends with them. She wants to kiss them. I sometimes want to punch them in the mouth. She wants to hold hands, and I don't want to touch their grimy hands." Her eyes met mine again, "They're sweaty."

Laughing together as we approached the car I asked her, "So you have already held a boys hand?"

"Not the way you think, but yes and I don't care to do it again for a while. At least not until they grow up. Maybe someone your age would be better to hold hands with."

I opened the car door for her, "I hate to burst that bubble Samantha, but when guys get goofy over a girl their hands still sweat."

She rolled her eyes and got into the car. I glanced over at Raquel, "Make sure she gets into the movies okay?"

"She will be fine. You don't have to tell me how to be protective."

"Try to have fun Samantha."

"Goodbye Kam."

I shut the door and watched them drive down the road.

Later that night when Samantha got home she came down to torture me. I heard the pounding on the door for a good three minutes before I could get out of bed and to the door. She's so giddy that she bounced on her heals when I opened the door. Her enthusiasm radiated off of her as she rambled, "Kam, why did you make it seem so bad? It wasn't bad at all, and I found out that Timmy likes me not Bri."

"Timmy?"

"Yeah, we have been friends forever, but I had no clue he likes me, likes me. This is so amazing."

"Yeah… Amazing." My words didn't sound excited like I wanted to be for her, but it's not in me to be happy about a boy liking Sam, and her being happy about it.

"It was weird, because when I went to get popcorn he moved closer. Then when I moved over to put more butter on it he came with and help push the lever. When we made our way into the theater he waited for me and let me move in first."

Trying to keep my distant from her, but she pulled me to the love seat with her as she fell into it and me along with her while she continued to rambling, "And then when we watched the movie he leaned into me."

She moved to sit next to me facing forward and leaned her shoulder into me, "Like this."

Oh shit, she's soft, sweet, and delicate, "So you had a good time?"

"Yes!"

"You like this Timmy boy?"

She moved away from me and turned so her eyes locked on mine, "No, not really. As a friend yes boyfriend nope."

My temper is growing deep within, "BOYFRIEND?"

"Kam! It's not as bad as it sounds. It's not like he tried to kiss me or anything."

"Did he?"

"No Kam. He asked me to be his girlfriend."

I swallowed hard realizing I need to make this okay even if it's torture for me. "You know it will happen someday."

"Yes. Not with him or any of the boys from school. It's because I knew them all when we were kids competing together. I can do the barrels and steer tie better than all of them. How could I like anyone I can rope better than?"

This girl could make me laugh, "You have a point. Does your mom know you came down?"

She glared at me, "Yes, why?"

I grinned and stood up holding my hand out for hers. She took it and I pulled her to her feet. I lead her to the door, "I will walk you up to the house."

She let go of my hand as we went out my door, but I could see a grin on her face. We walked toward the house. She opened the door but whispered back at me, "Your hands aren't sweaty Kam. I like that."

She closed the door behind her. She doesn't get that all of this is pure torture for me.

37 Prom

    Prom night for Sam will suck for me. Whose crazy idea was it for me to help chaperone? That's right I volunteered so I could keep an eye on her. So here I am standing in front of a mirror staring at my reflection where my suit hangs on my body. A clean shave and a new haircut made me resemble a dork. Not going to happen. Shaking my head upside down brought me back to being myself along with my crooked smile. One shot of cologne and a last glance I headed out the door and to the main house. I took my time getting ready so I wouldn't see Sam in her dress because I didn't want to torture myself. Avoiding torturing myself at all tonight, I promised myself I wouldn't search her out, and I'd comb the corners keeping young lovers apart at the dance. Once they leave the dance they are on their own.

    The night turned out to be exactly as I planned. No, Samantha anywhere that I've been, checking the corners and the outside parameter has proven to keep me from the torture I am avoiding. Raquel told me I should at least say hi to Sam, but my want to club her and bring her home is filling my mind more than once tonight. Seeing young couples kissing made my imagination run wild with what Tyler will try with her. If I witness him touching her or his eyes wandering over her body I would…. NO! NO!! It's up to her what she does tonight.

    Turning around a corner to head in my eyes landed on her. She's leaving with Tyler. I watched her coming down the steps admiring her taste in dresses. The dress she had on made her appear ten times older than she is. It's off white layered in lace which complimented each step she takes. The top is a halter covered with lace that traveled up to her throat and off her shoulders. Standing frozen to the spot watching as her hair swayed the same as her dress while they made their way down the steps heading out. She laughed letting me witness how happy she is tonight without me.

Tyler took her hand in his and my feet moved me in her direction. When he opened the car door for her my steps increased to a jog. After closing her door he sprinted to the other side and got in before I got there. First time in my life I wanted to face my desires up front and stop her from leaving with him. I ran my hands through my hair felling helpless. What the hell did I let happen?

Nothing could help me now laying here in my bed listening to Adam and Tracy in the other room. It's making me sick that I can't say anything to Kyle about his lovely daughter and the little jerk off that he hired to help me. I tried to drown out the sound putting ear buds in my ears and turning up the music. When that didn't work I covered my head with a pillow, and still no relief. The sounds of the squeaky bed, the moaning, the grunts, the growl of satisfaction, kept my mind on sex even though I tried to clear my head. My thoughts flowed to Samantha in that dress which made her seemed untouchable, like an angle.

She is untouchable, so I pictured her standing in front of me facing away from me. How I wanted to run my hands down her sides to trace every curve she's growing into.

STOP! I can't think about her like this!

I reached out to unzip the back of her dress; ambling down noticing every inch of smooth skin being exposed.

Maybe this is okay because I'm not touching her. I'm admiring her with my mind and a lot of space between us.

Carefully pulling one side of the dress off her shoulder I stepped closer.

I cannot stop myself from imagining the touching. Maybe just a...

I moved closer pressing my lips to her shoulder. Her weight shifted as she leaned into the kiss and tilted her head allowing me more access.

Oh, how I wanted to experience her warmth surrounding my desire.

I traced my fingers inside the back of her dress along the zipper allowing her time to adjust to my touch. Moving upward until I reached the material covering her shoulder sliding it off. Hunger to have her; my mouth came open to her neck tasting her as I moved closer.

I opened my eyes glancing down to see how bad it was because I now throb with desire for her. Ashamed, I put my arm over my eyes and stroked slowly as my thoughts went back to her telling myself, *this will have to do for now.*

Moving closer her hands came to my hips pulling me closer as she ground into me. My strokes escalated. Picturing my arm snaking around her body enveloping her body to mine I circulated my palm against her perk little nipple. Breathing became hard making my mouth dry, so I tried to moisten my mouth and swallow as my other hand traced further down until I caressed her.

Coming to a halt when I thought I heard something. Not wanting to be caught pleasuring myself I waited listening for the sound again. No sound came and relief filled me thinking, *Tracy and Adam are finally done?*

There it is again. Coming to realize it's someone knocking on the door. I sat up straining to listen even closer. *Did Kyle figure it out that Tracy is down here? How am I going to explain why I haven't told him?*

The knocking came more determined as I crawled from my bed and pulled on jeans. It will hurt forcing that arousal in jeans, but if it's Kyle I didn't need to be embarrassed. I grabbed a t-shirt and pulled it over my head on my way to the door. I rubbed my eyes as I opened the door if Tracy will get caught at least I'd be able to say I didn't know because I was sleeping. Frustration came out when I opened the door, "What?"

My tone carried anger I directed at the person interrupting my time with Samantha. At least the time I had concocted in my brain. To my surprise, Sam stood here in front of me as perfect as she was when I saw her earlier.

It's like my prayers are being answered as I stared into her eyes wondering what I should do. My mind flashed back to every thought I had about Samantha in the last hour. I wanted her to kiss me to not let me push her away.

Surprise apparent on her face as she spoke, "Sorry, I just wanted to tell you, you look nice tonight."

The moaning and bed squeaking started up again, and I rolled my eyes with embarrassment.

She pushed by me, "What is going on in here?"

"Sam, don't. You don't want to know."

"Tracy?"

I nodded.

"You can't stay here. That is awful."

I laughed, "Yeah, and that's not the worst of it. You're so… grown up, and beautiful." Reaching out to her I traced my finger along her face taking the patch of fallen hair tucking it behind her ear.

She beamed as the smile came to her face, "Kam, come with me for a walk to the stables."

I felt guilty about what I had been doing before she showed up, "Sam, I really shouldn't."

She's so stubborn, which is what I hoped for, "You would rather stay here and hear that?"

"No, but I shouldn't…"

She took me by the hand pulling me out the door.

"Sam, just a minute, let me get some shoes."

She crossed her arms, "I'll wait out here. Hurry up."

Going back in I grabbed my tennis shoes slipping them on and a sweatshirt. Rushing back out of the shack to catch up with her I put both my hands in my pockets as we started to walk with her.

"So, what are you doing home already?"

"I told Tyler I didn't feel good, and that he had to bring me home."

"You're sick?" That is not what I hoped for.

"I'm fine. I just told him that."

We both laughed as we made our way to the stables. Asking about every part of her night in search of what she experienced. Hoping she had a good time, but her answers continued to be short. Turning backwards to explain the dinner, swirling in circles as she talked about the dancing, and then she gave me at least ten expressions when she showed me the faces she made when they were getting their picture taken. Once she clarified she wasn't in on the parting I got the relief I needed. Enthralled in her voice and her night I didn't realize where we walked to. She could tell me anything and I would listen to her.

When she stopped we glanced around the hay room. Quickly I grabbed a blanket spreading it out on a bale of hay for her to sit on. She smiled, picked it back up, and laid it down on the floor. I gave her a disapproving glare and picked it back up. I grabbed hay and through it out. She grabbed more and threw it down. I grabbed a hand full and threw it at her and then she did the same. We played till she was full of it and so was the floor. I stopped and walked over to her, "You are a mess now."

She picked it off of her dress as I stood there and watched. When she noticed that my eyes stayed glued to her she moved to grab a second blanket spreading it out. Following suit I spread the one I had over the other one. She sat down and picked the straw from her dress. I sat down next to her and helped with the removal of all the hay. She laid back, and I shook my head. I'm in for it now and I couldn't stop myself. I lay down on my side searching her dress for more straw I could pull from her, "So, you had a good time."

"Kam, I wish it was you with me."

I'm so happy to hear her say that. No, she needed to be around people her age. Pulling back a little I took a deep breath to keep my composure.

She noticed my withdrawal, "Okay, Kam, let's just look at the reality of this."

I raised my eyebrows and blinked a few times. She is way more mature than even me sometimes.

"We have fun together all the time. We agree on things..."

Shaking my head no trying to disagree with her no matter how correct she is.

"Most of the time we complement each other with our knowledge. We talk a lot and I have to say you are more interesting than Tyler."

She does make me laugh.

"You respect me as a person, except when you treat me like a kid."

I couldn't help but let the smirk come to my face with guilt.

"Kam, don't you have anything to say? Aren't you going to argue with me? Come on, Kam, you wouldn't have had to kiss me, but you did."

How could I argue with her when I am so happy that she is here with me and not in a hotel room with a guy that would disrespect her? I took a piece of straw and tickled under her chin waiting for that beautiful smile to come back. There it is. Not stopping myself I leaned down dusting my lips against her for the briefest moment before pulling away. She's so perfect and beautiful I didn't want to tarnish that.

She raised her eyebrows, "Kam, I believe you kissed me."

Not agreeing with her I shook my head no, but the grin on my face told her otherwise. Not wanting to speak for fear I might tell her I love her I remained silent.

"Kam, can you tell me a story. I love your stories."

Laying back to think for a minute because I wanted to give her one she's never heard before. The perfect one came to mind as I took a deep breath, turned back to her, and traced my fingers along her cheek, "Okay, but you have to be quiet and patient."

"Okay." She's eager to listen.

I couldn't keep the smile from my face as I started.

"Well, there was this girl once."

Her eyes got bright with anticipation.

"I had a crush on."

She nodded but didn't say a word.

"Well, we hung out all the time. We watched movies, talked, exercised together. Well, I guess you could say we spent a lot of time together."

"What did she look like?"

I raised my eyebrows to scold her for speaking. She took her fingers and pretended to zip her lips making me laughed at her gesture.

"Okay, she was very typical to everyone else, but she was the most beautiful girl I had ever seen. Even at a young age she was amazing to watch."

"How old were... oops."

Chucking with the thought that inpatient's is typical for her, "Doesn't matter. So anyway, I had these feelings for her that came from my gut. Do you know what I mean?"

Placing my hand on her stomach, "Right here deep down you know that they're it for you."

She nodded and bit her lip.

"Well, every time she would come around me I would get this need to tell her, but every time I kept it to myself."

"Do you think she liked you?"

Raising my eyebrows I gave her a scolding glare.

"Oops, sorry."

"Back to your original questions, she's beautiful with long sandy brown hair but the bluest of blue eyes."

"Like me?"

"Yes, but that's what everyone looks like around here, don't they?"

She nodded, "But she was beautiful to you?"

"Yes," I raised my eyebrows, "She was more beautiful than anything I had ever laid my eyes on. She was young but so was I. We continued to hang out for years being the best of friends, even though I wanted to kiss her. I didn't know how to tell her. I would decide to tell her and then she would come around and I would chicken out."

"Why? You lost her forever because you were scared?"

"She was perfect and I am not."

She traced her hand along my face, "What happen?"

"I grew up and now I have responsibilities."

"So, you still have feelings for her?"

"Yes."

Her expression changed to dislike, "Oh." I could tell she was thinking about this, "You should try to get a hold of her if you still like her."

I shook my head grinning.

"What? Don't you wonder what would happen if you would tell her?"

"All the time."

"Is that why you won't kiss me?"

I leaned down with my mouth close to her ear, "Yes, but the truth is... it's you." I pulled back to see what she thought about this.

The tears were filling her eyes as she stared at me.

"Sam, I am sorry. I shouldn't have told you."

She shook her head, "No, Kam, I am happy."

Now that I upset her, I pushed myself up putting my head in my hands. Have I made another mistake? When her body move in behind me wrapping her arms around my waist up to my chest the warmth of her hands heated my blood to a boil.

"Kam, please don't be angry. I have needed to hear you tell me that so bad."

She kissed my back and traced her hands to that spot in my stomach I was telling her about. "Right there, Kam. That's where it is for me when I am around you."

I turned to her a little, "Are you sure, Sam, because I shouldn't have told you."

She gave me that sweet little comforting smiled, "Kam, you know that I have wanted this for a long time now."

I nodded, "But you know this is wrong, Sam?"

"Why? Why is it wrong to love each other? I am 18 now so it's okay for us to feel this way."

"Not really. There is eight years difference and I know what people will think."

"Kam, we will set them straight. You have always been a gentleman, more than any boys my age."

She cupped my face with her precious delicate hand and I grabbed it kissing her palm. She moved replacing her hand with her mouth. Her lips came to mine open and willing to kiss me deeply. This time I didn't stop, and I let myself taste her moving my lips in between hers. I gasped and went in for more than the taste of her lured me in for more. She moved to be in front of me and she pulled my sweatshirt off. I didn't pay attention until I had to quit kissing long enough for my sweatshirt to come over my head. Realization hit me that this was going way to fast, and I had to stop this. Before I refused my shirt was coming off too. It was still wrong no matter how I felt. Her lips came back to mine as her tongue touched my lip just before her mouth met mine. Oh shit, this is not good, but its soooo good. I wrapped my arms around her pulling her back as I lay down. I felt her body against mine and I was living my dreams. This was what I thought she would do. Did I want her to do this, and that is why I told her. Shit, we have to stop. Oh my god did she feel good as she rubbed against me. Desperately needing more I gasped again and moved my lips to her. Unzipping her dress before I could talk myself out of this I rolled her over and pulled it a little from her shoulder moving to kiss her there. She reached and kissed my ear as I sucked there for a moment. I stopped and looked at her. She smiled and reached to kiss me again while I got lost in tracing my hand down her side pulling her closer as I pressed my body to hers.

I had to stop this, and I pushed myself away from her sitting back up.

"Kam?"

"I can't do this."

"Did I do something wrong?"

I turned back to her taking her hand in mine, "No, not at all. You're just so perfect and I can't do this."

She was angry with me and pulled her hand away, "So you won't make love to me because you think I am perfect, Kam? Is that what you are saying?"

I nodded grabbing for her hand again to kiss it. She pushed me away and stood up, "That is what you are saying?"

"Yes, don't you understand? I am in love with you, but this is wrong."

She zipped her dress up and gave me the worst look I had ever gotten from her. She turned and walked out. I grabbed my shirts pulling them back on at the same time I was chasing her out of the stables. She was running with heals on. I got outside, and she was too far from me, "Sam, don't you understand. I can't because I love you."

She stopped and turned around, "You can be such a jerk, Kam."

Lost in confusion I didn't know what to do, so I watched her until she appeared in the light of the house. Heading back to the stable to clean up the mess we made. I kicked myself the whole time I cleaned up. Thinking that same thing; *what the hell did I just do?*

38 The Jerk

Thinking about Samantha's bad mood it's easy to remember all the times she called me a Jerk. It had to be at least a dozen times.

The first time was shortly after I came to the ranch. She wanted to ride so badly that day, but my time dedicated to the chores that needed to be done.

I went to feed bin filling the bucket.

"Kam, after you're done feeding the horse can we go riding?"

"That's going to be hard to do if they're eating. Wouldn't it?"

Huffing her disappointment she followed me to each stall observing each horse. When all the horse had gotten their food she skipped ahead of me turning in front of me, "How about now?"

Grabbing the hose I held it up for her to notice while turning it on. The squint of her eyes told me she didn't like my plan to fill their water buckets. Following me step for step until every bucket has water.

She ran back shutting off the water, "Now can we?"

It's not like she doesn't get that I do this every day.

Her persistence to ride and determination to get my chores done is going to blow up soon.

Each stall held a lead rope and reins, so I grabbed a lead heading into the stall of the first horse I fed. Hooking the lead under Page's chin I led her out and to the pasture gate.

Sam eagerly asked, "Can we go now?"

Shaking my head no I walked back in heading to the next one. Samantha started to irritate me with, "how about now?

Next one can we ride, this time Kam? How about now? When can we go?"

Not only getting irritated I roared at her. "Samantha, NO! I have work to do!"

She stopped dead in her tracks facing me, and put her hands on her hips, eyes full of tears, and screamed at me, "You can be such a jerk!"

The second time that I can remember is when I was replacing a section of fencing. She insisted on helping me and nagged until I allowed her to come with me to the back of the property. Driving about 8 feet, getting out of the truck to toss the supplies I needed at each post, and repeating it until all the supplies lay out. Beginning with the furthest out fence post I made my attempt to hold and drive the screw in at the same time. It's a balancing act at best so I asked Samantha, "Do you want to come here and hold this up for me?"

She did stuff like this all the time and I didn't expect her to get distracted so when I screwed the first screw in and the board moved it irritated me. "Samantha, help me out here."

More determined to concentrate we tried again. This time it slipped worse than the first time. It's going to take me months to get this done with her assistance. This time I yelled a little, "What the hell Samantha, if you're going to help then pay attention!"

Her expression changed instantly, and I knew I made a mistake by yelling at her. Though her chin lifted in determination, her eyes told a different story. In the depth of her eyes I witnessed the pain in her heart.

The strength she has comes with her ability to express her anger, "If you'd pay attention to your surroundings you would have seen what I have. LOOK OVER THERE!"

Taking a peek at what she's talking about just in time to watch a herd of deer dodge away with a few fawns following.

"You are such a big jerk that now you scared them away." She threw down the board and took off at a run towards the house.

The third time she called me a jerk happened to be the day I told her father that she's a pain in my side.

Fourth time a dinner where Samantha is going to announce important news. I got busy with one of the animals. One of the horses has twisted intestines, so I had to keep him up until the vet could arrive. Torn between the news Samantha wanted to share with me and taking care of Poco. If I understand Samantha like I thought I did she would be thankful and understanding. When I finally I made my way to the house dinner was over, so I walked into the kitchen searching for Samantha. Raquel watched me enter and pulled a plate of food for me from the fridge and put it in the microwave for warming, "You might want to avoid Sam for a few days."

"She's that mad?"

"You could say she wants you gone."

Raising my eyebrows, "Does she have any idea of what I was doing?"

"Yes, but you have become very important to her and when you didn't show, she didn't tell us her big news."

"So you can't help me with her?"

"Nope. Hey, you good? I need to go up to bed."

"Yeah, I will be fine. I'll take the plate down to my shack and bring it back in the morning."

"That sounds good."

When the microwave pinged notifying me it's done I pulled it out set it on the counter and then got a glass out of the cupboard. Pouring myself a glass with the door open to save time and almost dropped it when the door closed and Samantha stood there with a blank expression. To ease the moment I said, "Poco will be fine."

That's when I got the glare; cocky, full of feistiness and disgust all rolled into one.

"So what's the big news?"

She raised her eyebrows but didn't answer.

"Samantha, don't give me your attitude. I don't deserve this because I really do care about you and everything else here."

Her eyes glimmered with tears, but her stance changed to attack, "You think you know me, you think you know what I feel. You can be such a jerk sometimes." That's when she left me standing there speechless.

The fifth one that I remember is the time she entered in the science fair. We just got in a couple more mares. I needed to get them set in the stalls with hay, feed buckets, and water buckets so the time got away from me.

She stormed into the barn yelling for me, "Kam! Where are you?"

Not trying to hide from her I let her know, "Sam. Over here with Lacy." Restless this one is, and I tried to calm her down, but she didn't want to settle down. There is no way I'd leave her like this. I wonder if horses can have space anxiety. Samantha found me right away and even decided to help me with Lacy, but didn't say a word to me. My suspicion is that she is so mad at me that she's not going to talk to me and she is here to show just how angry she is.

"So how did it go?"

"It's no big deal."

Instantly my heart went to her. With that attitude she didn't do well, and I empathized with her. Intending on cheering her up, I complimented her project telling her, "It's a good invention. Your dad even mentioned it to me as a plan for here on the ranch."

Nothing. Not a shrug, not a pout, and not even an evil glare. What is going on with this girl? She ignored me.

"Sam, you shouldn't let it bother you."

She shrugged her shoulders.

"You shouldn't be so hard on yourself."

She still didn't say anything to me. My heart ached for her pain. Have a need to make everything better I walked up behind her hugging her from behind and whispering in her ear, "Just because you didn't get an award doesn't mean it's not good."

She turned to me eyes full of tears, "Do you really think that I am upset about the stupid project? You don't know me at all. It's not about the project or how I did. What hurt me about tonight is that you didn't come. You can be such a jerk." Storming toward the door she stopped shy of leaving. Not turning back to me, but yet speaking at me, "By the way... I got first place."

Wanting to hug her and apologize, I took two large steps toward her, but she bolted out the door before I could reach her.

The longer I sit here the more times I remember her calling me a jerk. Okay, so maybe I am a jerk and didn't even see it, but this is so different. I am in love with her so it's out of respect that we wait not me being a jerk telling her she's not good enough for me or something stupid like that. This last year has had a lot of ups and downs so the last thing she needed from me is sex.

When and if it happens I want it to be perfect for her. I want to take our time, explore each other, and bring her to that place where there is no turning away from, a love so deep that we touch each other's souls leaving the mark of forever. Loving her so much I forced myself to stop. That's respect in my mind. How is that being a jerk?

Horse Play

39 Depart

After the other evening telling Samantha that I am in love with her it's clear I will pay for it through daily blasts for turning her away. That is the maturity level of her age and I understand that, but I don't have to like it. One can never tell how much torture she may attempt or for how long she can stay angry with me.

Heading to the barn for chores it's not surprising that Samantha has already come down and started without me. Avoiding the argument, I worked on my own chores and chancing a glance once in a while. No matter the fear of what she's capable of doing I find myself drawn to her watching her every move. Flinching with each change of direction as if she's would charge me with a shovel, or whip me with a riding crop. She wouldn't do something so crazy like that but a woman scorn you never know what will make them crack.

I about jumped out of my skin when she spoke.

She asked, "Where is Adam?"

She already knows the answer to that question so she will try to make me jealous using Adam, "I guess he will be down in a while."

"I am helping 'till he gets here." What is she up to? I replied with a short answer, "Okay."

I watched her rake out a stall bringing the hay to the center of the alleyway so we could shovel it into a wheel barrel, but she didn't stop to help me with that part. She grabbed the new hay and went back in the stall spreading the new bedding. Watching her every move, I waited for the explosion but nothing, not even a glare. She is being cold-hearted, as if she doesn't care about me one bit. Deciding that this punishment isn't so bad so I asked, "Sam, can we talk about last night?"

Without missing a beat she stalked closer until she stood directly in front of me eyes boring into me, "No."

That's it. She didn't want to talk about it at all so she turned around leaving me stand here with an ache in my chest. Questions filled my brain. *So why did I love her? Why would I even want to love her when she acts like this? I did it for her. It should be in a castle or on a cloud, or I don't know. Where would you make love to an angel? A very stubborn, strong headed, pain in my butt angel.*

After the early morning chores were complete I headed up for breakfast. When I entered the room everything and everyone seemed normal. Eating and discussing today's agenda. Even Samantha talked about the day ahead like she had no plans for beating me up more. Avoiding direct eye contact, I watched out of the corner of my eye, and even twice through my eyelashes when I needed a better picture of her in my mind.

Surviving breakfast without a verbal hit, a visual glare, or a blunt kick in the ass I went back to my chores thankful that the situation hasn't escalated. Hoping for her appearance I went to work with the yearlings. I didn't think she could resist the temptation to help. I still wanted to be around her as much as I could. She's like an addiction for me more so than any food or drink, but what I have to realize is that she is out to torture me for pulling myself away from her so I didn't get carried away. Not all men can do that and this is the thanks I get for being a good guy. She's making me worry without being here, or that's part of the torture.

When I got a glimpse of her she was following Adam around. If she's trying to make me jealous she's mistaken, because he is getting everything he wants from her sister. Stifling my laugh with a huff she glanced over her shoulder at me pretending she didn't see me at all. I know what she is up to and it will not work.

Picking chores that would keep me near I listened to her ask him questions, but his answers were hideous. When she rolled her eyes with disgust I felt the need to head out of there before I break out in a full laughing fit. There is no way she would put up with someone who is that clueless about horses.

Letting the horse graze in the fields is my agenda today so one by one I walked them out to the gate giving them the freedom to roam. Samantha can put on a show when she wants to. Walking in once she had her eyes set on Adam in Awe, the next she giggled, a few times later she full out laughed. I kept my cool until I saw her on her tiptoes wiping the sweat from him forehead.

That's all it took for me to blow my even temper. Not giving them the opportunity to see me coming I grabbed Samantha around the waist throwing her over my shoulder heading to the grooming area. I didn't let her go, even though she kicked and screamed the entire way, until we were in the room with the door pulled shut. Holding her face in my hands, I let her know she will not win this one, "If you think you are making me jealous enough to do *that*, you have another thing coming."

That pout came out with her jaw set to stubborn, "What am I doing?"

It's wrong to want her, touch her, to even think about her this way but I love every inch of this girl and I cannot refuse her with those eyes gazing upon me full of tears. I wiped my thumbs against her cheeks while explaining, "I told you I love you and that is why I can't take that next step. You deserve better than me. Why can't you see that if I can? And you choose him to make me jealous? He's sleeping with your sister."

The tears spilled out of her eyes before she shoved my hands away from her so she could get away from me. I wanted to stop her, but I'm not sure I could stop myself from kissing her hoping to make those tears go away. Watching her run back to the house tore at my heart more each time she leaves me. How can I make her understand just how much I love her?

"Kamron, is everything okay?"

Hearing his voice I closed my eyes as my heart dropped to my stomach. I rummaged for something to say, but the only thing I could think came out, "I think I have to leave."

"After lunch you will meet me in my office."

Nodding in agreement he walked away. As if my time would be up I pushed myself to get more done, to get the paperwork in order, and just be ready for the end. Not wanting to eat at all going to the house seemed to be a waste of time, but if I'm leaving I have to see my Samantha one last time if I will spill my guts to Kyle.

Walking to the house with Adam I filled him in on things he needed to know in case I leave right after my meeting with Kyle. Being the first one to dinner after getting all cleaned up I noticed Samantha has not come down yet so my attention fell on Kyle. Shit, I like it here. Kyle gave me a reassuring grin gesturing for me to take a seat.

Lunch is quiet while everyone ate. I didn't have the heart to look up even after Sam came to the table. Afraid that if her eyes meet mine I wouldn't be able to leave her knowing how she feels. It would break my heart to hurt her this way. Right now she is angry with me, but if I leave she may never forgive me. *What the hell am I going to do?*

Running scenarios in my mind of what I will say to Kyle, so he will understand why I need to leave. I tried to come up with little white lies but nothing sounded genuine. The whole table carried conversation, but I didn't pay attention until Kyle spoke, "Kam, Raquel asked you something."

Glancing around the table first my eyes fell on Raquel, "Sorry, I've been thinking hard about something."

Now Samantha's eyes moved to me paying attention to what I have to say. Hum. When I don't want her to see how much pain is in my heart right now it has to show on my face.

Raquel asked again, "I'm wondering what your plans are here."

My heart stopped at that moment. Is she asking me if I intend on courting her daughter? No, that is not even possible, "What do you mean?"

"Well, you're the trainer here so what is next on your agenda."

Not sure if she's asking me indirectly if I'm staying or if this is as innocent as she's making it sound. If I stayed this would be the plan, "Well, I've been thinking I'd train Jack and Diane for a performance show so we can increase their value. I want to train another horse, maybe Pearl, for show jumping if we can find a rider."

Tracy jumped at the chance, "I have never done that. Can I try dad? I mean Kam, you will train with me won't you?"

"Yeah, if that is what your dad decides."

The fury of Samantha showed its head, "No, that is what I do. You can't do that. If anyone trains for a show it will be me."

The table went up in hysteric's as the girls argued while my mind wandered back to Kyle and what I need to say to him, what I need make him understand that this will not work any longer, because I love Samantha and she loves me and if we continue to spend all of our free time together this will go further. Not being able to face my agony I stood up and took my plate with me, "Excuse me. Kyle, I will wait in your office."

All the arguing dropped off when I left the room. The murmuring I didn't listen to, but Samantha's voice stood out, "Why is Kam meeting you in your office, Dad?"

I couldn't wait to see if he would tell her. It breaks my heart.

Making my way toward the stables trying to come up with something anything to make it right if I stay, but everything points at leaving to prevent things from getting out of hand.

Samantha came running while yelling my name full of hysterics. Turning in time to catch her throwing herself into me wrapping her arms and legs around me so tight, "Kam, you can't leave. Please tell me you will not leave me. I promise I won't flirt with Adam anymore. I promise I won't make you kiss me anymore or anything else. Please, please, please say you will stay. I am so sorry, Kam."

I held her tight not knowing how to reply, but when I could I whispered to her, "I think I have to go."

"No, you don't."

My heart hurt like pounding in my chest trying to leave my body and stay with her, "He heard me say I love you."

"I know. Last night when I left the stable he was waiting on the porch for me. We talked. He knows it's all me, Kam. I told him I loved you and I pushed you and you still wouldn't be with me. Kam, please tell me you won't leave me?"

"What am I going to say to him?"

"Anything, please tell me you won't leave me. We'll train Pearl and will go back to running and working out. If we stay busy we won't have time to get carried away. Then in the fall I'll have school in the fall so it will be easier than, right, please say you won't leave me."

I held her so tight knowing I'd give in to her pleas, "I will try, but, Sam, the way I feel about you is wrong and I know it's wrong. I am wrong and I shouldn't have let it go this far."

"No, Kam, it's not wrong. You have a family here and families work out their problems. They don't just throw them away, or run away when things get hard, they work harder to make things work. Kam, we can make this work and I promise I will behave."

Her hair smelled like lilac bushes, her skin smelled of musk. Between the two scents I wanted to kiss her, but instead I lifted her hair to my nose consuming her. I didn't want to leave, and I didn't want to let her go ever but I lowered her to the ground, "I will try."

She looked up at me and I leaned down to kiss her but she pulled away, "No, Kam, if it is hard for you then we won't kiss either. I love you, but until you feel you are good enough for me then we will wait."

I nodded trying to contain my desires for her.

She touched my face, "Dad said he would come down after I go back up. Do you want me to go?"

I didn't want her to leave; I only wanted to stare at her a little longer, so I shook my head no.

"What do you want me to do, Kam?"

I shrugged my shoulders.

She wrapped her arms around my waist and put her head to rest on my chest. I had to take slow deep breaths to calm myself. When she let go she glared at me, "Are you ready?"

Nervously I asked, "For what?"

"To talk to my dad." She searched my face for my answer but I didn't have one for her.

"Kam, families work out their problems. Promise me you will try."

I nodded as she reached up and kissed my cheek. I turned to kiss her lips hard and forceful. Pleased with her response to letting me devour her. When she pulled away I rested my forehead against hers, "I love you, Sam."

She smiled the best I have seen her smile in a long time.

"Then don't throw in the towel. Fight for things you want. I will wait for you."

She let go of me and ran up to the house. I went to the office and fell to the chair to wait for my fate.

Kyle walked in with a notebook in hand. He moved to his desk but his eyes didn't meet mine as he set the notebook down. He took his time preparing himself for this conversation as the sweat beaded all over my body. When he felt comfortable his eyes came up to greet me with an explanation, "I wrote some of the things you said you would like to do can you elaborate on your ideas? I want the specifics if you don't mind." He hesitated, but he's not done so I waited. He read over the notes he made and read out loud, "Now you said you'd like to work with Jack and Diane, what class would you put them in?"

What an odd conversation for firing me. Kyle caught me off guard, so I stumbled through my answer, "Um, pleasure. They're young so it would be good to get them in front of a crowd and display their class. Build a little name for your ranch with awards for producing award winning animals."

Raising his eyebrows he stated, "And a name for yourself as a trainer."

If I wasn't so focused on him I would have never seen the side of his mouth twitch with a hint of a grin. "How about Pearl, what should we do with her?"

Not holding back my grin I gave him my intentions, "I want her for the Equitation class. That's what Sam is best at so I would want Samantha to showcase her. She could be ready by next summer."

He nodded still holding that grin back, "Anything else?"

"Well we could work with Timber and Grey now if Sam would like to compete, or even Tracy if she is serious."

He smiled yet again, "So, with these plans why do you think you have to leave?"

There it is, the hit to my gut with a low blow. Now what do I say? He heard me tell Samantha I love her so I cannot deny it. Intimidated by my guilt I found it hard to meet his inquisitive stare.

Not waiting for me to reply he continued, "Hum, I think you need to hear a story instead of telling one."

That's demanding that I pay attention to him and his story. He must think that I took advantage of his daughter with the framed photos in my shack because he handed me a picture of a young girl on a horse. Her attire was more like a wrangler than a young woman, sort of like Sam. Not lady like with real cowboy boots on, a cowboy hat that looked worn. She held the reins in one hand and a lasso in the other.

Chuckling with the thought; picturing Samantha as this young woman. Based on the background I would guess it's her grandmother, or maybe even further than that.

"This little pistol could out ride all of us men and herd more cattle than us too. Her dad put her in charge because he said if she can do it better than the rest of us she's the boss. There were many that tried to out ride her, but she always put them in their place by the end of the day. The guys would talk about her in ways I couldn't stomach to hear. She's fifteen in that picture and they talked about her in ways that made my blood boil. What they'd like to do to her."

When my eyes met his I could see the fury in them. I'd feel the same way. I'd kill them if it were Sam.

"Well she tickled my fancy, so I seem to get in a lot of fights back then, but it wasn't until her father pulled me aside to ask why I got so many black eyes. I didn't have the heart to tell him but he understood belter than I could ever explain it. The weirdest part is he understood how I felt about his daughter. He pointed at her and said, 'That is my pride and joy, but the way you honor her it would be a privilege to have you court her someday'. At the time I was 23. The age gap back then wasn't a big deal, but for me it was hard because the way I felt about her she wouldn't have been ready for me. I'll tell you one thing though, the harder she rode the faster I fell for her. By the time she turned 17 I couldn't stay away and her kisses lured me deeper. We married before her 19th birthday, and we had Tracy when she turned twenty. When I look at my wife she has total control over me and my decisions. I would give her the world and everything in if it would make her happy, but do you know what she says?"

Glancing up my eyes met his in anticipation.

"She apologizes to me, because she loved me and I felt bad about her being so young."

I swallowed because that was my Sam in every way.

"The other thing she regrets is that she never gave me a son." He laughed when he said this but he continued, "I don't think I could have raised a boy to be like me. That takes dignity, integrity, and self-discipline. It is a special man that contains all three qualities and I see all of them in you."

I couldn't speak even if I wanted to now. The lump in my throat was blocking my air way.

"I think you have good plans here and it would be a great loss if you left. Will you stay?"

I nodded, and he returned my look with a smile.

"It takes a special man to love a woman that has made mistakes. I know you have loved her since she was fifteen, maybe even before that, but to love her even after the Jared thing; that takes a special love."

My eyes must have popped out of my head because he laughed, "Yeah, don't think you can keep secrets around here. Momma and me, we know everything."

I felt like choking but he stood up, "You have things to work on if you are staying."

I nodded and stood up to shake his hand but he came around the desk and hugged me, "You are family here. We would like to keep it that way," as he patted me on the back.

I went through the rest of the day in a daze. I thought I would get canned today and I think he's telling me he would like me to be part of his family someday. Was that what he was telling me?

Horse Play

40 Grown Up

Sam and I worked with the horses, Jack and Diane all year long. She stood in the ring with me as we both did the same movements together while having them performing in sync with each other. Pearl is on a lead now doing small jumps trying to make her comfortable with the jumps procedure.

Samantha's Graduation day didn't come fast enough for me but today is the day. I borrowed a suit from her dad to wear to the ceremony, not realizing it's not a formal affair, but for me it is the official declaration that Samantha is now an adult. Samantha doesn't get the signification of what this means because she still went on about her life clueless that her wearing a short black dress that flowed while walking down the steps toward me did things to my body and mind she doesn't understand. Forcing my thoughts to cleaning the stalls I held open her car door.

Before getting in she asked, "Are you riding with us?"

Not knowing how long I could withstand watching her with all her friends at a distance so I needed my truck for an escape. Shaking my head isn't the answer she expected from me. She turned to face me and traced her hands down my lapel, "You're very handsome today."

If I dared to show her my excitement for this day I'd take her face in my hands and press my lips to hers with the intent to never let her go again. Not in the real world so I grinned my "I've got a secret" grin and replied, "You are beautiful."

She wrapped her arms around my neck hugged me tight while whispering in my ear, "Thank you for coming with today. It means a lot."

"I wouldn't miss your last day of childhood."

Maybe it's my words that through her off. Releasing her hug she held herself away from me scanning my face for an answer of a question she didn't ask. No she didn't have to ask because her forehead scrunched, her eyes squinted, and her lips parted.

Not giving her a chance to ask I helped her into the car smiling with every word, "You need to go."

Everything about Samantha tells me she will be my better half, but it will be a challenge every step of the way. Her eyes glared at me through the window after I shut the door. Knowing she wouldn't give up that easy I'd have to explain my comment later.

When she walked up to get her diploma we stood and yelled. I don't think we should have done that, but Kyle stood up with me and then the rest followed our lead. The ceremony only lasted about two hours, and it's a done deal making the weight of loving Samantha peacefully lift from my shoulders.

After, we went out front to take pictures with her friends, parents, and her sister. Raquel is the one that pushed me into a picture with Sam. Comfortable as part of the family I put my arm around her shoulder and smiled for the camera. Samantha's eyes were on me so I turned to her. Our eyes stayed on each other with a promise that this is the first day of the rest of our lives together. The camera's continued to click even though we weren't smiling for the camera. That is until Raquel interrupted us with more family photos.

After that day we became inseparable, and I loved every day. We ran in the mornings before working, and she came to work with me every day. We did workouts before lunch, then with the horses in the afternoons. After dinner time we would find something to do together like going for a ride along the trails, or training horses. We worked with Timber and Grey most of the time. Tracy came down to ride Grey and Sam rode Timber. Sam and Tracy seamed to get along great, but in privacy Sam complained that Tracy is a horrible rider. I tried to remind her to be patient with her sister because she has not ridden like this before.

The summer is hot so we spend a lot of time outside at night. We sat on the porch of the house drinking ice tea.

Sometimes her parents would join us and sometimes they left us alone. It seems easier to be around her in this atmosphere now that I don't feel so guilty for being in love with her. We held hands and talked about the future of becoming a vet. She wanted her own practice specializing in horses. No surprise there. We talked about where she wanted to live with her making it clear she wants to stay close to her family. She went on and on for hours about how she wants it designed and how she would handle calls. I sat taking in every detail of her dreams as if I could see them myself.

She paused then asked, "Kam, what is your plan for the future?"

I didn't have a future that didn't involve this ranch, her family, and her. Wondering myself how I would take care of her I shrugged my shoulders. Not wanting her to realize that her plans outweighed mine I stood up pulling her to her feet with me.

"What are you doing?"

I have other plans for her tonight, "We are going for a ride."

Her maturity level changed the day she graduated, but tonight she giggled for the first time in a long time. Wrapping my arms around her we headed to the stables where I saddled up two horses and grabbed blankets. She allowed me to help hoisted her up and after getting up on my horse I reached out taking her hand in mine as we headed out down the trail.

"Don't you think it's a little dark to be riding?"

Wanting to be alone with her I shook my head.

We ended up at the creek where the moonlight is all we had to guide us. Her eyes stayed on me full of wonder as I laid out the blankets side by side. Next I pulled her down pointing to the blankets where I wanted her to sit.

Her eyes sparkled in the moon light, her face bright with delight, "What are we doing?"

Taking a seat next to her I explained, "We are waiting for a falling star to make a wish."

She laughed and laid back. Mimicking her move I lay down on the other blanket taking her hand in mine as we waited for our falling star. The quiet of the night filled my ears with nothing but my heart beat. My dream of having Samantha to love is coming true each day we spend together.

"Kam, I have one question."

"What is that?"

"It's official! I'm an adult now, so how come you haven't kissed me?"

I rolled to my side so I could cherish my beautiful girl, "Because, you are too perfect."

She rolled her eyes at me pushing me away. In her playful way I let her push me away. We stared at the sky for 15 to 20 minutes when it all started. The first meteor crossed the sky. The screech of delight filled the air.

"There, Kam, a falling star."

It's not a falling star. Having inside information that there is a meteor shower I had to share this with her. We spent the whole time with her watching them stream across the sky, and me watching her enjoyment of witnessing this amazing site. The bellows of delight stirred something deep within me. My imagination created a scene where she made those noises from the pleasure I created. Driving myself crazy with lust I needed to make her mine very soon.

Concern filled her face as she turned, "What is happening. It's like they are all falling."

Not being able to contain my enjoyment in her excitement I explained, "It's a meteor shower. It's supposed to last for 45 minutes."

She screamed with each one. I moved perpendicular to her resting my chin on my hands keeping my eyes on the one person I loved more than anything else in this world.

She glanced over at me, "Aren't you going to watch this."

"I see something better."

As the show lessened she turned to me again, "You knew about this in advance. You planned this out?"

"Yes, I did."

The night air cooler than I planned on so it was time to head back to the house I took her hands in mine pulling her to her feet, packed the blankets. After getting everything packed up I asked, "Can I ride back with you."

"I don't know. You do sneaky things."

While I laughed she unhooked the saddle from Timber. Not understanding her thoughts I asked, "What are you doing?"

"If we're going to ride together it should be bareback."

Rearranging the saddles we got on Timber together. Wrapping her with a blanket I took Gray's and timbers reins in one hand and Samantha's hair in the other as I lifted it to my nose. Whatever she uses for shampoo did things to my wild side and I took advantage of the proximity.

She leaned out so she could turn to see my face, "Why do you do that?"

I've done it so many times without her asking me why she surprised me that she noticed it at all, "What?"

"Smell my hair. You have done that before?"

Shrugging I replied, "Your hair reminds me a summer with a touch of vanilla."

As we headed back down the trail all my attention stayed on her tracing my nose along her jaw, nibbling on her ear lobe, and soft little sucks of her skin on her neck. When she freed my other hand from the reins and squeezed my thigh with her other I knew she likes how I make her feel, and she's giving me permission to continue with my teasing assaults to her body. Every muscle in my body reacted to her riding movement rocking us forward and back in a rhythm. I want more, no, I need more of her. My hand left hand wandered under the blanket, under her clothing, to the smooth skin pulling her tighter to my body. It wasn't until I breathed into her ear the same time my thumb grazed over her bra covered nipple that sent her into a low moan of pure ecstasy. If I hadn't been hard already that would have done it in a split second. Her free arm came up wrapping around my head as she leaned and turned giving me access to her mouth. Taking advantage of the soft lush lips parting for me I dove into her mouth with the need of the last 5 years. She needs to know that it will be this way every time she shares herself with me. Undoing her button on her jeans and unzipping her pants just so I could trace my finger along the edge may have been pushing myself too close to the edge. As she pulled away to catch her breath she gasped into my lips, "Kam, please make love to me." Resting my forehead to hers we stayed there for a few minutes to calm ourselves,, or maybe I did it so I wouldn't give into her plea because of how I need her right now. Her body tremble against mine and all I could think about is *it wouldn't be special*.

Flinching when her hand held my check and her fingers graced my lips while she pleaded, "Please Kam?"

It will not happen right now. Wanting to make it unforgettable for her I didn't want it to be on the ground, even though doing it under the stars might be something special but not for the first time. Taking every bit of strength I could muster up, I repositioned her in front of me and held her tight hoping to contain her need beneath the blanket I whispered into her ear, "No yet my sweet love. It will happen soon, but not today." Not only did she huff her disappointment I could feel it in her body as we resumed our path back to the house. It wasn't until we got close and witnessed Kyle and Raquel out on a blanket in front of the house that Samantha tried to put herself back together under the blanket. Guilt washed over me and I only hoped that her parents wouldn't be able to see my embarrassment.

"Samantha, do you need help?

Her laugh came loud and clear, "Oh Kam. I love you so much. I'm fine."

Brushing a kiss on her cheek I gave her my inner feeling, "I love you more than I can ever explain to you."

She leaned back into my arms.

41 Meteors

All the outside lights were out, and they were looking at each other until we rode up. Kyle turned to, "Where were you two?"

I laughed, "We were doing the same thing you two are doing."

Raquel laughed, "Meteor shower."

Sam's excitement exposed by her rambling on about what we saw. I lowered her to them before heading to the stables to put the horses away.

Kyle walked in, "Can I give you a hand?"

Nodding my appreciation for his help he took the extra blankets and saddles putting them away. When he came back in, he folded his arms across his chest, "So, how did it go?"

Why would he ask that question? It's a little weird he'd want to know anything about us together.

His chuckle brought me back to the current time as he asked, "Did you figured it out yet?"

"Figured what out?"

He shook his head, "Wouldn't it be easier if you got it over with?"

Was he telling me to sleep with his daughter? Talk about awkward. I don't even know how to respond to that.

"It's time to ask her to marry you."

I coughed, "Yeah, shouldn't we go on a few dates first?"

He laughed, "Right, like a few dates will help you make that choice. It is written all over your face, and Samantha hangs on everything you do or say. Those kisses aren't so innocent either."

"Does she talk to you about that?"

"No, she talks to her mom and mamma tells me everything. So, what is your problem?"

Not wanting to talk to her father about us, so how do I explain that I want to make her toes curl? I can't believe I'm having this conversation with her father. Taking a deep breath I replied cautiously, "She is too perfect and I am getting comfortable with it."

"Getting comfortable with what?"

He wants details? Leading Timber to his stall I tried to escape the questioning.

"Kamron, what is it?"

He wants me to go into detail? Shit, "She is so amazing it will take me a while to get comfortable with her being an adult after years of putting up those walls. I still see her as a little girl asking me a million questions and when she touches me I pull away out of habit. It makes me nervous."

He laughed and nodded, "But does she know how you feel? That you are in love with her?"

"Yes, I tell her."

"Well, that's a start. She is a lucky girl to have someone love her that much, and I am a lucky father because you show more respect than any man could handle. With you... I can trust that my daughter special to you. You are a good man, Kam."

I laughed and took Grey to brush him. He stopped me by grabbing my arm, "Do you ever think that you don't deserve her?"

Worried about what he said I stood there frozen staring at him.

"Don't pass up the opportunity to have a relationship because you don't think you are worthy. You've proven time and time again that you are worthy of her. Remember that when it come times to ask her to marry you."

Kyle hit the spot that worried me, "I have nothing to offer her."

He grinned and shook his head, "You love her. That should be enough to start. We didn't start here like this. We took years to get where we are today, and we did together."

Me and Samantha building a life together sounded perfect.

Kyle continued trying to convince me, "Kam, Raquel's family had money not mine. I was the hired help and her father helped me get started. All I had to do was come up with a good plan and when I did he supported my plan. What you need to offer her is your love, and that is more than most. Now days, people get married because they are pregnant or because they get caught up in the convenience of a relationship. You two, it's different. I believe that you love each other and that can build an empire. Look what it did for me, but the thing to remember..."

So far all his advice has been good. Turning my eyes met Kyle's.

"Woman like attention, more attention, and even more attention, if you show her she is the most important person in your life everything else will fall into place."

When I laughed out loud he pat my back with a heave hand and headed out of the stable. Following Kyle a few minutes later I took Samantha by the hand and walked her to the front door. Her sweet little smile twisted me into knots, oh how I wanted to taste those sweet lips again. As I leaned forward I whispered into her ear, "May I kiss you good night?"

Her little fingers gripped onto my shirt as she pulled me closer, "You need not ask, Kam."

Pushing a wayward curl back behind her ear, "Yes, I do. Is that a yes?"

As soon as she nodded I cupped her face in my hands and touched her lips with mine carefully. Her need is far worse than mine because she moved her mouth against mine with greed. When her hands traced up my sides things became firmer as my longing grew. Grabbing her hands within mine I removed them from my body and pulled them in front of us.

That twelve year girl flashed in my head when she stomped her foot at me, her lip came out in a pout, and she complained, "Kam, what?"

I pulled her into my embrace hugging her, kissed her cheek, and spun her around in a circle. When she let go she laughed asking, "What are you doing?"

"I don't want you to be mad at me, but when you touch me like that... it drives me crazy."

She laughed and tried to touch my waist again like a game. Her playfulness is full of flirtations seeing a side of Samantha I haven't seen previously. Her eyes glimmer with need, her mouth playful and pouty, and the rest of her body now in full woman mode stirred my cravings even more. It's a good thing Kyle and Raquel approached us when they did, or I may have snuck her off to have my way with her. Her parents caused enough of a distraction for me to take advantage wrapping my arms around her trapping her arms. Now she is at my mercy so I moved her out of the way as they walked into the house Kyle stopping just inside the door. He turned to us with his deep voice saying, "Sam, say good night to the boy. He still has to work in the morning."

Replying for her I said, "She will be right in."

Kyle gave me that knowing grin when he nodded his good night.

Sam turned grabbing my shirt again, "What is going on with you and my father?"

"Nothing."

She glared, "You will tell me why he grins at you like that."

I raised my eyebrows, "Maybe someday."

She went for my waist again but I opened the door and shoved her in all while she hung on me and the door frame trying to not let me win. When she realized she wasn't making any headway she stopped pushing her way out.

Happy that I won I wanted to make her happy too, "Sam, can I take you out for dinner tomorrow?"

With the smile on her face I knew my answer before she replied. When she said yes she came at me fast and kissed me long, hard and deep on my mouth. She left me breathless as she moved away from me and closed the door.

42 Fantasies

How am I going to fall asleep with all this energy pumping through my veins? Samantha makes my heart race faster than my mind can go. There has to be a way to prove to her father that I am the man he believes me to be. Samantha deserves the best and I will be the best person for her. I just need to find something that will allow me to be great. How am I going to come up with something when my mind keeps wandering to her?

Samantha's eyes on the sky as the first meteor streaked across the endless blackness. Watching her emotions play on her face as another one flashed across the sky. The happy squeals of excitement escaping her mouth as she anticipated the next. Where my mind took over the reality starts with those lips. It's like she is here when I reach over tracing my fingertip along the ridge of her lips boarding her skin. Her mouth parts for me, but she doesn't stop there. Her tongue slips out to moisten her lips, but makes contact with the tip of my finger. My manly parts twitched with need as it stiffened. Anticipation did wait long before her lips wrapped around my finer as she sucked it into her mouth. My whole body shivered as I shook my head intending to rid myself from this fantasy. This girl is going to be the death of me without even trying.

I rolled over moaning to myself and pulled the pillow over my head. Having this fantasy is not going to help me in any way so I have to stop imagining Samantha this way, or I am going to drive myself crazy.

It wasn't long before my thoughts went back to the blankets. The time as I watched her I traced my hand along her waist. It distracted her from the sight of meteors falling long enough to cup her hand to my face. I pulled up her shirt enough to expose her navel. I moved closer, and closer, I wanted, no I craved her. Her watchful eye, accepting everything I want to do. I blew a breath over her and glanced up in time to watch her eyes close in delight. I moved closer hovering above her skin blowing a breath across her stomach. Whimpering made her stomach shutter. That is when I couldn't take waiting any longer so I positioned myself between her legs and licked and open mouth kissed her right above her belly button. She arched into it as her hands came to hold my head to her.

Shit.

Sitting up in my bed refusing to give into what my mind led me to. With these ideas I am never going to get sleep. I rubbed my face as I got up to take a cold shower. Killing these thoughts with a cold pounding shower is the only thing I can do to relieve the pain I'm in right now.

43 Reality

She wasn't only in my thoughts but in my dreams too. Dreaming about the ride back to the house with her in my arms is more PG rating. I smelled her hair, traced my hands along her arms, and with my legs rubbing against hers.

Her whisper came, "Kam."

The same as the ride her saying my name that way made the smile grow on my face knowing what she will say next.

Her voice more determined to get my attention, "Kam."

I turned my head toward her voice finding her standing next to my bed. This fantasy will be better than the last and a lot harder to get through. She's dressed in a camisole, silky shorts, and a robe that hung open for me to see what is beneath it. Oh yeah, I don't think I will control where this one is going. This hallucination better than any dream my mind has concocted before. I reached for her hand to see if she felt as real as she looked. Yes, it does. It is so real I shot up as if the bed is on fire, "Is everything okay?"

That sweet smile soothed me, "Yes."

Relaxing back into my bed relieved, "Did you need something?"

Please say yes, please say me.

Her eyes glistened, "I wanted to say thank you for tonight."

A little weird she wanted to say that tonight when she could tell me this tomorrow. This is so unfair of my brain to create another scene with her playing the lead role in my life. This is a dream, it has to be. I replied, "I'm glad you liked it."

Her grin grew to mischievous. This has to be a dream when she orders me to move over.

Glancing up at her not believing what she asked me to do, "What?"

She rolled her eyes, "Move over, Kam!"

I shook my head. I had to get these thoughts out of my mind or I will get no rest. Confirming my suspicion of this being a dream when her fingers tracing over my body and then pressing to my chest. I didn't want to refuse, I wanted her to want me; and I wanted to give into my dreams. When both hands pressed on my chest my blood rushed to meet her hands with warmth. The sensation didn't last long as she crawled over me. Torn over being tortured by another dream and wanting to let it progress into ecstasy.

"Samantha, what are you doing?"

Her eyes full of concern she replied, "Showing you."

I shook my head, "Showing me what?"

That's when the cute little flirty smirk came to her face, "Just how thankful I am."

When she leaned down her mouth and lips grazed my chest, every inch of my body tense with anticipation. It worried me that this wasn't a fantasy, but it has to be. Not wanting to know the truth I gripped her legs that straddled me, "You don't have to thank me Samantha." But I liked this idea. Her nipples now pressing against her camisole were distracting me from looking at her innocent face. I have to stop this. My mouth dried with the quickness of my breath. With every ounce of control I forced my eyes to meet hers, "I like to see you happy."

She raised her eyebrows, leaned forward, "I am happy now." Her body pressed against mine as her lips traced my neck. I will give into her any moment if she keeps this up. She worked her way to my ear. Before I felt her lips her breath caressed my inner ear driving me insane. Grabbing her by the waist we rolled over with me on top of her. She's making me hard as nails. Propped myself up on my elbow I traced my other hand along her face, "Do you know that you are the most beautiful woman in the world."

Her giggle sweet, innocent, and fascinating all confirming that this is a fantasy because there was no trace of fear in her eyes this can go even longer because of it. Temptation took over, and I rubbed the palm of my hand against the nipples that push against her camisole. Hearing her moan a little my eyes moved back to her face where I saw her enjoying my touch.

This will be so much better when it's real; I only hopped that I can withstand the torture of the fantasy until then. I captured her mouth with mine to contain her noises, but even with my mind I cannot make her noises stop. It was those noises that made me want to check. Moving my hand down her front until I could reach beneath her shorts and panties where I played with her clit until her hips rose in need. Covering her mouth with mine I consumed her moaning with my mouth as I became more and more hungry. I had to stop this now, because I'll end up torturing myself for thinking about Samantha this way, and embarrassed to let my eyes fall on her.

Pushing away I rolled to my back in need of getting her off my mind.

Her voice soft and trembling, "Kam, it's okay. I love you. Make love to me please."

Her words put a smile on my face, but it's only my brain playing tricks on me so I'd continue with the fantasy. And by the pain that throbbed between my legs I will need to do it soon.

"Are you laughing at me?"

I shook my head, "You are my fantasy."

"Kamron?"

As I glanced over to her the sadness of her face proved her anguish. Tracing my fingers along her cheeks as my brain filled with thoughts of pleasing her, "I have to stop fantasizing about you now, or I will not sleep at all."

She took my hand and pulled it to her. Pushing it back to where her wetness called to me, "Does this feel real to you Kamron?"

I pulled away and sat up staring at her. She's real and we just... oh shit, ooohhh shit. What the hell am I going to do now? "You have to go! NOW!"

Her eyes filled with tears as she pulled the robe around her. The expressions on her face were flowing from one of hurt, to being pissed off. "What is the problem?"

I pushed myself from the bed and looked back at her, "This. It's not the right... it's not the way... shit Samantha." I paced. She bolted out of the bed and out of my bedroom. Following her I grabbed her around the waist before she got to the door. I pulled her wrapping every inch of her body with mine. Her sobs wet against my shoulder as I caressed her back. I didn't mean to lead her on, or get her so turned on to push her away. After all the fantasies I've had I believed this to be the best one ever. Holding her tighter I stroked her back until she calmed. Glad that the shock took away my desires because now I'm calm enough to just hold her. When the sniffles stop and she relaxed in my arms I released her intending to see her face, but she hugged me tighter. This night had been glorious, but because of my hang-ups I ruined this special night for her. We stood there holding each other that my body reacted to her and the way her body's curves melted into mine. Not wanting to go down that road again I tried to get her attention, "Samantha?"

She squeezed even tighter. I took a long deep breath and moved only enough to grasp her face in my hands so she'd gaze into my eyes. Those blue eyes so pure, innocent, and full of wonder; how is it she had done this with my nephew? No wonder he got carried away because I could get lost in them forever and be fulfilled. Denying myself I closed my eyes while pressing my forehead to hers. How am I going to put this so it makes sense to her without hurting her again? The only thing I can think of came out my mouth, "I am so in love with you."

Her body trembled against mine, her breath heavy, and then a whisper back, "Then why won't..."

Unable to explain with words I captured her mouth with mine, leaving no room to question my want or need for her. My heart belongs to her, and every part of her belongs to me. "Forever," escaped my mouth as my lips pulled her deeper into my assaults. With discomfort I pulled away growling my irritations of having to stop this now. This time when I opened my eyes to meet hers the blue magnified with tears wrenching my heart tight with regret. The tears brought on by need she took a step back her eyes staying on mine as she spoke, "You touched me deep within my soul. My need as obvious as your own..."

Her hesitation didn't mean she's done, so I waited. When her eyes squinted with ferocity a lump in my throat grew.

The soft touch of her fingers against my check didn't lesson the determination in her eyes as she finished her sentence, "Don't ever do that again, because I won't come back if you push me away one more time."

She's wrong. I'm not trying to, "Sam, I wasn't pushing you away; all I'm doing is asking you to wait, because I want it to special for the both of us."

Her hand came to my mouth to stop me from finishing. Her eyebrows raised and her cantor grew stronger as if she was her mother. Now I can see why Kyle gave that woman anything she wanted. Samantha reached up kissing me on my cheek and spoke firmly, "Perfect? It was perfect. It might have been more perfect if we made love. I can only handle rejection so many times Kam, and this will be the last."

She walked away from me and my heart fell to the ground. I want to be the man that satisfies all of her wants and needs, but I have to do this my way. She will understand someday.

44 *P.S.*

Standing here lost as Samantha and her parents pulled out of the driveway on their way to drop her off at college. Regretting my choice of not asking her to marry me before she left for school is eating at me starting in the gut. Wanting to kick myself in the ass for stalling the vehicle disappeared in the cloud of dust. I have three months to get my shit together so when she comes home I will feel good about asking her to marry me. Adam tried to distract me from my thoughts, but nothing will distract me from what I need to do before she comes home. My heart aches already, and my mind wonders where it shouldn't, hoping those three months of college life will not change her mind about me.

Thinking about her my heart continues to hurt every day while every meal is a reminder she's gone. My gut is giving me so many issues I carry a bottle of Pepto around and even drink this with dinner. Kyle and Raquel asked questions and encourage me to see a doctor, but all my stomach aches and pains is from missing Samantha, and the worry of losing her to a hot young college guy that will give her what she wants. If it's not my stomach gurgling it's my mind driving me mad. Staying busy is my only comfort so I work from sun up to after it disappears at night. Exhaustion cures my mind from fantasizing about her because when my head hits the pillow my mind shuts down. The relief only temporary as each morning approaches and my brain rests in that in between state where it creates a half dream.

A month after she left a letter came from her. Kyle walked it down to me right after he picked up the mail. When he handed it over I didn't look at him. I walked away to my shack staring at it. When I got to the table I set it down staring at it. Something is telling me not to open it. Fear set in as I stared at it. If she wants to talk she'd call me. A letter is old fashion, and there is something about a letter that reminds me of a *Dear John letter* to say your goodbyes.

A knock on the door took hold of my attention bringing me to the here and now. Kyle stood there with a grin saying, "Are you coming up for dinner?"

Dinner? It's just after 2 p.m. The mailman always comes at two. Kyle glanced over my shoulder again asking, "It's time for dinner and Adam said he hadn't seen you since I brought you Sam's letter."

Three hours of staring at an envelope with my name on it. I am not one to get so hung up on a woman or be this insecure, but she is the only one for me. Changing my attitude is what I need to do. If it's not meant to be then it's over and there's nothing I can do to change it. *Shit!* Three hours later and I haven't gotten any closer to opening it. Glancing back one more time I headed out the door with Kyle.

Kyle must have noticed I hadn't touched it because he asked, "So, what did she send you?"

Embarrassed I grumbled out, "Don't know."

"Why haven't you opened it?"

"I am afraid."

His eyebrows furrowed, "Of what?"

Not sure if I want to admit this but it came out my mouth anyway, "That she has grown up and found someone better."

"After dinner do you want me to come down while you open it?"

I shook my head, "No, I have two months to open it."

"What if you are supposed to write her back?"

I chuckled, "Okay, I will open it after dinner."

He patted me on the back as we went in for dinner. They had a glass by my plate but it was empty. Not under I looked around and everyone else had milk.

Raquel spoke as she noticed my confusion, "We didn't know if you wanted the pink stuff or milk."

I laughed as they all lightened the mood.

When I made it back to my shack I sat down at the table again still worried that this is my Dear John letter. In my head I'm already planning on the next move. Where would I go, what would I do? After opening the envelop I pulled the letter out.

Scanning through the letter I searched for I love you but... the words I'm sorry aren't there. She talked about how hard it is to share a room with someone she didn't know, the social events that the school puts on so they meet other students, and her classes. What I found interesting is she feels that high school did not prepare her for the real world and college at all. We laughed together as she explained her roommate's behaviors. If I know my Sam, she will be the boss of that dorm, and no one will stand in her way. She went into a little more detail about the roommate how City slickers just didn't get the natural order of things. The roommate is there for the fun of it, but my Sam is all about business. She has goals. When I finished her letter I sat quietly remembering why I missed her so much. Folding it back up I found a PS on the back of the second page.

Kamron,

I know you think I am perfect and precious, but I am far from that. Remember my mistake a few years back? Well, I do and you were perfect. Once you see you are everything I want then maybe you will realize we are meant to be together. Please wait for me. I love you.

Samantha

Think of what I'd say I pulled out a note book to write her back. Keeping things light I wrote about the ranch and how everything is going. I kept it general but when I got to the end my p.s. entailed saying;

Add I thought I would have to ask for you to wait for me. I love you, Kam

Thanksgiving came bringing Samantha home. I rush from one task to the next working to get everything done before she gets here so I could spend every moment with her I can. My name screeched through the air finding its way to where I stood in the last stall. Tossing the hay in my arms to the ground I exited the stall intending to head up to see Samantha. When I stepped out of the stall she hit me full body jumping into my arms. I held her tight as I took in her scent. You would think I am obsessed with her. Well I have to admit there was something about this girl.

She kissed me hard and long and I couldn't help but smile with her embrace. I opened my eyes to watch her, but she had her eyes closed. I moved my lips so I could taste the sweetness I missed.

Every time she came home we were inseparable. We went to movies, dinner, walks, riding, and hanging out talking. I could tell she's getting more mature as time goes buy but I could also tell she is growing out me. She didn't make me feel stupid or anything and she asked me more questions than I even understood, but she asked because she wanted my input on things. Summer came after her spring break which we spent laying on a blanket by the creek. I had saved enough money this time and now it's time to make things right. This time I waited on the steps eager to help move her back in to her room. As she got out of the car I walked up grabbing her bags as Kyle grabbed totes. She took my hand as we walked into the house. I laid them on her bed and turned to her, "Will you go riding with me. I need to talk to you."

She gave me the best smile but then it disappeared, "Is it bad?"

I shook my head, "No, I just missed you."

She followed me out and down to the stables. I saddled up one horse as she grinned, "Kam, one horse?"

I peeked under Grey at her, "Yeah, did you want to take two?"

She walked over, "I haven't ridden for a while. Do you mind?"

More than happy to oblige her need to ride realizing she must have missed it. I saddled up Pearl for her. Samantha traced her hand down pearl's nose while asking, "How are Jack and Diane?"

"They are great. You could enter a competition this summer if you would like?"

"No, I am done with competing."

"Really, so we don't get to work on things together anymore."

She smiled and traced her hand along my face, "We will work together for the rest of our lives Kam. We'll just be doing something different than we used to do. You will train and I will take care of the animals."

I laughed and continued to get Pearl ready. Hoisting her up she gazed down at me with a huge grin watching me move to Gray.

I chickened out on asking her to marry me, but I enjoyed listening to her talk about school, her studies, her new friends, and her new needs. The only reason I chickened out is not a good reason, but she's out growing me and I'm not sure how to handle it.

Horse Play

45 The Trust

She headed down the trail slightly in front of me and a little to my right. When she glanced back at me with that mischievous smile it brought me back in time...

I yelled to her as she took off down the trail, "Samantha, come on! That is so unfair and you know it. I don't know the layout yet."

Now at a full run on a horse I didn't trust yet is not my idea how to start a job. This child will be a pain in my ass. When I got to the meadow and didn't see her I pulled back on the reins deciding I'd check the property out on my own hopefully I'll find my way back.

Dismounting, I walked along the fence that seemed to be deteriorating. This is something I must fix soon. Out of the corner of my eye I glimpsed her approaching. Not wanting her to take off again I continued to walk along the fence counting what I needed for supplies to fix this area. That's when I decided to mark the posts with reads of grass. Samantha seemed to sneak up on me, but I continued with marking the posts. This little girl and her horse play will get on my last nerve.

Keeping my chuckling to a minimum as she tried to move closer hiding behind trees, but she had to see me laugh. Did she think the horse couldn't be seen behind the trees? She leaned so far out from behind the tree she almost fell off the horse earning a loud laugh from me. That has to be the cutest thing I have ever seen and if she wasn't such a pain in my ass I'd find her irresistible to fall in love with her

When I got to an area that seemed all right Samantha was nowhere to be found. It's time I take advantage of this powerful animal. One last check around the meadow to confirm she must have gotten board with me and went home. This is my chance to get acquainted with this giant horse called Saber. First, I removed the saddle then lead him around intending on earning his trust. Walking and leading him to the right, to the left, a full circle, and then the figure eight until he responded well to my lead. Saber is a Friesian so his body is strong and sturdy, he walks with elegance, and he has a brain like a stallion. During our walk I spotted Samantha again, but when her eyes met mine they filled with question. It's time Saber found out who is the boss between him and me. Focusing on Saber I moved to lunging. It's an effective way to make a horse respond the way I want them too. It's easy to do, not bad for the horse, and just a control tactic that works. This tactic builds trust wile dominating the control. Samantha reappeared, but seemed to be irritated with me or my way of training, but I continued with the lunging.

Once confident in his trust I glanced around for Samantha before moving to the next thing I wanted to work on. Samantha lay on her stomach watching us from under the fence.

This is as much about taming the child as is about the horse. I moved in circles directing the horse reverting to lunging to remind him no matter the situation I am still the one in control. Samantha moved in closer and closer until she made her way next to me.

Not surprised when she spoke, "I know what you are doing."

My mouth twitched with an avoided grin, "Really? What am I doing?"

Stopping her foot at me, her eyes glaring deep into my soul I wondered if she understood how young she is, but with a tongue like hers could tear anyone to pieces, "It's called lunging, but he is already broken, so you need not do this. Do you have any idea what you are doing?"

In her stubborn way she's challenging me so I continued with the movements while she mimicked every move.

I chuckled, "Yes, I do. Do you?"

She glared up at me, "Are you telling me I am wrong?"

"No not at all. I am building the trust with him."

"Why?"

"Because he we haven't had the chance to get to know one another, and I want him to understand that when I direct him in any way he should obey me because I am the boss."

"No you're not. I am!"

Handing her the lead I walked away, "Your turn. You show me how to handle him."

I went to the fence and leaned against it. I didn't want to go too far for fear he would give her some trouble, but she didn't need my help. The first thing she did is wrap the lead as she approached him. She let him smell the rope in her hand while she stroked his forehead. It's like he is meant to be her horse. She turned glancing back at me and moved under his head hugging him, "See, he does just fine."

"Can you direct him to do anything you want? Try lunging him."

She smirked and rolled her eyes, but will she attempt to direct him the same way I did? Again she took charge lunging at him. His reaction didn't surprise me when he pulled his head to the side. This tactic is for the person in charge of the horse. Saber no longer knew who he should follow instructions from so he stumbled and got a little too close to Samantha so I rushed back out to her side halting him from doing any damage. The confusion showed in his eyes as he backed away from us.

When she looked up at me, her eyes wider than normal, "He didn't like that."

Comforting her I said, "He will not like it. It's putting you in charge, and he is a little uncomfortable with that. I felt it when I rode him out here. But I want him to trust you and you to trust him and this is one way to teach that."

She looked back at him, "But we already have an understanding. We need not do this."

Patting her on the back I replied, "Trust me. You will like what I have in mind to teach him, train him, and develop him in a way to make him an amazing horse to ride in a show."

I had only been here for a week and she hugged me around the waist. What do I do with this? Well, I didn't have to wonder for long before she shoved me away, "Fine! I guess you have a point, but I don't like that he is afraid of me."

"He's not afraid of you, it's different and he's not used to it. It will get easier each time because he will learn what to do to make you happy."

She walked over to the horse she rode out here with, swung up to the saddle with ease, and headed down the trail at a gallop.

Hoping my jest would stop her, "Samantha, quit with the horseplay will ya? I want to find my bed sometime today."

I heard her laughing with her reply, "I guess you better catch up than."

She glanced back with the mischievous smile as I got on Saber and released him to go as fast as he could carry me.

Comparing her back then to now isn't much different. She liked to egg me on and I took enjoyment in irritating her. I chickened out of asking her to be mine for the rest of our lives for no apparent reason. Thankful to have the afternoon with her by myself is the only distraction I needed to forget why I asked her to be alone with me. She's growing into a woman far more intelligent than me bringing doubt to my head. Even though it's apparent that she loves me very much. It's all in her kisses.

46 Company

I woke to pounding on the door. Adam came out at the same time I did. He looked at me with a sense of panic on his face. I shook my head showing that I didn't know what was going on either.

"Kam, come on open the door."

I went to the door and open it to see Jarod standing there in front of me with a suitcase in his hand. I didn't know what to say or do, but this wasn't what I needed right now.

"Are you going to leave me out here or can I come in?"

I opened the door turning to watch him as he walked in further. Adam was still standing in the doorway to his room.

"I see you have a roommate now?"

"Yeah. What are you doing here?"

"Dad and I got in a huge fight and mom gave me some money to come stay with you until it blows over."

"You can't stay here."

"You're throwing me out?"

"No, but after what happened before I don't think it's a good idea for you to be here."

"I promise I will stay away from the girls, especially Samantha."

Adam laughed, "So this is your flesh and blood and you gave him the same speech you gave me. Hah, and what is this about Samantha?"

I turned to Adam and glared, "None of your business. Go back to bed."

He walked more into the kitchen, "No way, I want to hear this."

Walking over, I grabbed him by the neck, "In your room now or I am talking to Kyle tomorrow." Turning to Jarod I directed, "You can have my room, but you are not allowed out of this shack." I pointed my finger at him, "Do you understand me?"

"Yeah! Yes, no problem. Can you tell Samantha I am here? I would love to talk to her."

"After the last time you were here, no, I can't and won't and neither will you. Her dad has an idea of what happened last time, so no, you cannot see her."

"Okay, okay, but maybe after a little while. After I prove myself as decent guy can I?"

Adam came back out, "So he doesn't have a clue what is going on here?"

I picked up a pillow off the couch and threw it at him, "Get out."

He laughed going back in his room. Jarod walked closer, "Tell me what?"

"It's nothing."

"It's about Sam?"

"Yeah, I mean no. It's nothing and I have to get up early so we will catch up tomorrow and you can fill me in on what your dad is so mad about."

He laughed grabbing his bag, "He caught me with a girl in the living room."

I wanted to throw up. I grabbed his shirt, "You stay away from Sam."

"Fine, but if she comes to see me I will not hide."

I pushed him, "You are not to go out of this shack. Do you understand me or you are out on your ass?"

"Fine." He huffed at me and went to my room.

I paced around the table and around the couch making a figure eight. I had to talk to Sam to warn her he's here. How was she going to act? What would she do? She had sex with him... would there be any possibility of her still having feelings for him? *Shit... shit... shit. Dam that little shit.* After pacing for two hours I decided that I had to go get Sam. Finding Jarod snoring, I headed up to the house. It surprised me to find the front door open so I let myself in and went up to her room letting myself in. As I approached her lying in her bed I realized that I am crazy for even coming in here, but I'm already here so I had decided to wake her to discuss this new situation. Letting my fingers glide across her cheek she startled sitting up alarmed. Covering her mouth with my hand, I sat down whispering to her, "Shhhh. It's me." I curled my fingers gesturing for her to follow me. Her robe hung on the back of her door so I grabbed it and wrapped it around her. We grasped hands as I lead her down the steps and out the front door. Holding hands, we made our way down to the barn. Her smile had mischievous written all over it as we entered the barn. After closing the door she wrapper herself round me when I turned to her. Not wanting to push her away I let her kiss me while I showed her that I want this and her, but not right this minute so I growled my displeasure as I pushed her back a step. Backing her up until she had to sit on a bale of hay, I paced in front of her wondering how I'm going to get to the subject of this encounter. Concern showed on her face as I paced back and forth.

"Kam, it's obvious you didn't bring me down here to kiss, so what exactly is going on?"

I stopped walking and looked at her, "Um..." I went back to pacing. How am I going to bring this up?

"Kam, you are scaring me. What is going on?"

I ran my fingers and hands through my hair and moved in front of her staring into her eyes. I swallowed the cotton ball in my throat before trying to speak again, but as soon as I opened my mouth everything went out of my brain.

"Kam, what?"

Not being able to face her I walked to the doors of the barn, looked out the window, and blurted it out, "Jarod is here."

There is only one thing I need to hear from her. Please Sam say something, anything that will tell me you hate him. As I waited for her to say something my nerves grew agitated.

The tension relaxed when her hands trace my back. When I turned she cupped my face in her hands, "What is he doing here?"

Not the response I hoped for. "He got in a fight with his dad."

"So, how long is he staying?"

Shit, this is not the way I wanted this to go. "I'm not sure."

"Did you tell him about us?"

Shaking my head, I replied to her, "Us, what about us? I don't know what to say."

"Say you love me, or is that what the problem is?"

Gripping her hands in mine, I shook my head in disagreement, "Sam, there is something I planned on talking to you about, but now... are you sure?"

"You know why I was with him. I didn't think you loved me and he was the closest thing to you I could get."

Embracing her I held her tight to my body. She filled every need with one sentence. Tears come to my eyes as I gazed into hers. Resting my forehead on hers, "Are you sure? I mean really sure Sam. He is more your age and I would understand... I mean you have been with him."

"Kam, stop it right now. Don't even go there. I am in love with you like I have always been."

Hold my feelings back my body trembling as I took her in with my breath. I replied with the only thing I could get out, "Okay."

I saw a smile come to her face as she stared into my eyes.

47 The Flirting

I couldn't sleep after getting back to the shack trying to find comfort on the love seat. Every which way I turned I didn't fit. When I found a comfortable position my eyes fell on Samantha's picture. How am I going to explain this to Jarod? He will think that she's settling for me because she wants him. I know that is what he will think and I don't think I have the heart to tell him otherwise. Dealing with them last summer is my nightmare that repeats in my head.

Their first meeting is when Samantha sat on Bruno and we did jump training. Bruno, the youngest colt on the ranch is beginning his training. Directing him from the ground Samantha applied body pressures to teach him what they meant. Jarod and Samantha hadn't met yet but Jarod called from the side of the ring, "So what do you want me to do now?"

I glanced over, "Go grab something to eat we should be done here in a little while." Glancing back at Samantha to see her attention on Jarod made that irritation to grow.

"S A M !"

Jarod didn't want to listen either. He climbed up the Fence perching himself on top to observe our training. With Samantha not following directions and Jarod showing signs of interest I cut practice short. I had to get them separated, the girls are off limits to the help and it is my job to keep it that way. Not really but I feel it's my responsibility. Sam got off Bruno and over on the fence with Jarod before I knew what was going on. This is not okay.

"Samantha, Bruno needs to be cooled down and brushed."

She waved me off like horses aren't important to her.

"Samantha!"

Her attention came back irritated with me, "I KNOW!" But she didn't move from where she sat then they laughed about something she said. That is it; I will not allow it her to treat me disrespectfully, so I walked over with Bruno in hand and gave her his lead. Grabbing Jarod I pulled him down to his feet, you both have work to do.

I've never seen Samantha this way. She's giddy, goofy, and acting like a regular teenage girl and I hated seeing her this way.

The next time I caught them together is when I had Jarod cleaning the stalls. Samantha watched from the gate. They didn't talk, so I didn't want to make a big deal of it, but when I walked by Jarod he worked without a shirt on and Samantha stood there drooling. I rolled my eyes and went to get Bruno ready. It's time for training so I should have said something but I didn't and now I have to go back in and get her. When we walked out to the ring she remained quiet. I thought for sure she'd be made at me for pulling her away from watching Jarod, but not a word.

"Are you ready for today?" No reply, no groaning, no nothing. "Samantha, we're working with Cavellettis today. Are you ready for that?"

She's not listening, "Oh forget it." Still not responding to me, so when we got to the ring I handed her the lead, "Just put him away."

She glanced up at me, "Why?"

"You're not listening and you're not in the frame of mind to work hard."

I walked away. My heart couldn't take seeing her wanting him. Being with someone her age is better for her, but not for me and it's breaking my heart though it's the right thing to let this happen for Samantha.

Not making it all the way back to the barn when she pulled me to a stop, "What is your problem? I'm ready!"

I crossed my arms over my chest and raised my eyebrows. Not having the heart to explain to her I didn't like the way she acts around Jarod with that hurt and disappointed look on her face. Not that I wanted to, but I caved, "I think you would rather do something else."

Her voice escalated, "Instead of working with YOU?"

Does she understand that I see her and the way she is watching him and now she's upset with me because I am giving in to letting her spend time with him? Heat pounded through my veins so my replay may have come out a little harsh and I meant it, "Yeah!"

She stepped closer, "You know I am not a little girl anymore!"

I glared, "So... If you don't want to train then don't. Just don't take up my time if you will act like that."

"Like what Kam?"

This is not happening, so I turned to walk away from her. I will not argue about her being a teenager and me being a man. It wouldn't happen. Ever! "Samantha, I don't have time to put up with distractions or the silly, goofy girl stuff. Either you want to train for the next competition or you don't. No skin off my chin."

"IT FEELS GOOD!"

Not understanding what she is talking about I came to a halt and turned to look at her, "What?"

"The way he pays attention to me makes me feel like I'm pretty, and like I am a girl. Not just a student."

I rolled my eyes, "Samantha, you are way to…" Not sure of the right words I searched my brain. She's been so emotional lately that I will regret anything I say, but here it goes, "You're more mature than that; to act like a young girl in heat."

Steam may have come out her ears as her eyes squinted in irritation though she nodded. We stood staring into each other's eyes neither one of us wanting to cave to the other one, but when her eyes filled with tears my body slumped in submission to give her whatever she wants or needs. Oh Hell I am in trouble here, "So you want to do training now?"

The happy face I love and cherish reappeared on her face as she grabbed my hand and pulled me to the ring for training.

The amount of times I caught them alone talking made me worry about how attached they are becoming. They sat swinging on the porch swing talking between the two of them. I could see Jarod's hand and Samantha's hand close enough to touch. I didn't like how close they were getting, and I remember laying out the rules when Jarod got here so he should respect my wishes. Driving up to the house rolling my window down I yelled, "Jarod, we have work to do."

He yelled back, "Okay." But he didn't move.

My anger grew watching him linger with Samantha, "JAROD! NOW!"

It took my yelling to get him to move, but he did something I didn't expect catching me off guard. He bent over and kissed her on the cheek. It didn't last more than a second, but it's about all I needed to lose my cool. He came running while Samantha moved to the top of the steps to wave to us as we drove away. Every inch of me grew warm as my blood boiled beneath my skin, "You know the girls, Samantha to be specific, are off limits."

He laughed, "It's not like that."

He will blow me off like that when I am so pissed that I am having a hard time keeping my shaking hands on the steering wheel. However, my mouth acted on its own accord with voice that is not mine, "What is it then?"

He laughed more, "She is just nice, and a friend. I like to talk to her. She helps me see things differently, and she is cute."

That did not help my anger, "I told you the girls are off limits!"

The laugh he bellowed out filled the cab of my truck. He is not helping to calm me down.

After the porch I saw them together all the time. Sitting on a blanket in front of the house, riding together, even when Jarod worked she'd tag along with him. And now I will tell him she only did that to get to me. How could I break his heart like that because it broke my heart when I found out they'd been together? It will have to come out clear. She is the love of my life and I am hers. She is mine and soon to be until death do us part!

48 Wronged

Getting Jack and Diane ready for a training session I brought them to the riding rink. Starting with simple tasks of walking together, trotting together, side stepping together but things are not going as planned. I worked on getting them to synchronize their movements with the thought of Samantha and Tracy riding them together in a companion but it's a lot harder than what I had originally planned on. Working the routine I had in my head only worked for Jack. Diane didn't want anything to do with me or Jack. When Samantha wandered down towards the ring I smiled to myself. This could work if I could get Samantha to help out with Diane, or help with Jack so I could work one on one with Diane.

Sam climbed up the gate getting ready to jump down when I saw Jarod come running and jumping up to talk to her. All the ways she might tell him I only hoped that Sam will be careful I repeated in my head over and over, *Sam please be careful with his feelings.* Preoccupying my time training with Jack and Diane I kept the corner of my eye on them. The more I notice Samantha and Jarod, the more Diane put a fight. The conflict in what I needed ad what I wanted forced me to ask for Samantha's help. Only when I turn to ask Jarod had Samantha's hand in his. What is she saying to him that would make him move in on her now? Shit, is she trying to make me jealous? Of course she is, and it is working one hundred percent making my blood boil and my body shook fiercely

Diane grunted with disapproval and I forced her to follow my lead. Jack tried to back away, and I held him firm. When I glanced back over they faced each other and spoke more intimately. My throat tightened while I forced the two horses in a circle again probing for higher steps at the same time. The next time a I glanced over Jarod traced the back of his hand against her cheek. That's it, "SAM!"

She smiled and said something to him then jumped down jogging out to me. The funny thing is she is glaring at me when I am the one that had to watch her flirting with Jarod. He scolded me when she got near, "Are you having issues?"

"Yes."

"You are supposed to guide them not force them Kam. Boy, I wonder who taught me that idea." Her eyes rolled with disgust, but her glare featured the green that pierced my soul.

Not wanting to discuss my training I shook my head determined to find out what happened, "Well?"

"Well... What?"

"Did you tell him?"

"No, you are going to tell him, right? This is going to be a little difficult."

My heart rose to my throat, and I wanted to scream at her. Jealousy is not good for me. "So, what did you talk about?"

She walked up to me her eyes meeting mine, "Are you jealous?" She pulled two carrots from her pocket and fed one to each of the horses. Another trick I had shown her. She grinned mischievously.

"Sam, please?"

"He asked me why I told you about the pregnancy scare and not him."

"What did you say?"

"You are my best friend and it only seems right to confide in you."

Moving in front of me she took Diane's lead and walked with her a little calming the animal. Following her lead I led Jake in a circle and then went through some moves which Samantha copied with Diane. All the issues Jack and Diane had this morning vanished. They performed in perfect unison. Glancing over at Samantha, I grinned at her until I saw Jarod on the fence behind her so I yelled to him, "Don't you have chores to do to earn your keep?"

He laughed, jumped down, and replied, "Sam, we have to talk later tonight."

My attention went straight to her. She shrugged her shoulders at me but yelled out, "Yeah, sure. See you later."

He waved, and I moved closer to her, "You are encouraging him."

"No I'm not. I just need to blurt it out to him that we're together."

"No, please Sam. We have to be careful about this."

"So it seems, but how do I tell him that I wanted it to be you all along?"

My eyes fell on hers finding the color deepening within them. Then the tip of her tongue came out to moisten her lips. There is nothing I want more than to make love to her. Her cheeks grew pink while seeing my need grow deep in my soul. Wanting to wrap my arms around her and pull her to me to taste her soft, and sweet lips. I shook it off and said, "Sam, I do have a question for you."

"What is that?"

"Why did you do it with him? I mean really, truly, and deeply why him? And why didn't you tell him?"

She walked up to me pulling Diane alongside as if trying to hide us. She touched my face gently, "Kam, there wasn't any chance of pregnancy. I've been on birth control since I was fifteen."

I stepped back wondering why she lied to me, "But you were upset and confused."

"That's why I said I didn't want it. I wanted to make you jealous hoping you'd do something about the feelings you have for me. I've been in love with you and I did it with your nephew to make you angry and tell me how you really felt."

"You are a manipulative, controlling, self-center girl. I don't understand why you'd do something like that."

Tears filled her eyes from the hurt I caused her and she took another step closer, "Kam, please don't hate me. I only wanted you to react and show me how much you love me. It's always been you that I love. In fact the only reason I did it in the first place was to make sure I'm good enough to satisfy you."

"That is the stupidest reason I have ever heard."

She through the rains at me and took off running.

"Sam, wait. Please there is something else I need to tell you. Please."

Jarod came out of the barn running after her and I stood there like an asshole as Jarod wrapped his arm around her shoulder. Shit, *what have I just done?*

I went up for dinner knowing Jarod did not follow my orders to stay away from Sam. I walked in to find Jarod sitting next to Sam at the table as they spoke softly. Kyle glanced up at me raising his eyebrows to ask me a silent question. He must be wondering why Jarod is here or why Sam is being all mushy with him. Without a word I sat next to Adam with my mouth shut and my eyes on my plate. She's trying to make me jealous and angry because of what I said earlier, but I am not going to participate with her manipulative behavior. If she ever allows me to explain what I meant I tell her that it's supposed to be special with someone you love. That's what makes it good. Even though she was stupid for doing for the wrong reason it's still wrong of me to say it the way I did.

"Kamron!"

When I looked up everyone at the table stared at me, but Kyle seemed to be fuming. If I stayed here I might blow my temper, so I gave the table a half hardy smile, stood up, and shook my head, "I don't feel good today. Please excuse me?"

Putting the napkin on the plate and then I walked out not wanting to hear or see Sam and Jarod together. It brought too many memories of them together and sometimes it's too much. She knows I love her with all my heart now so why would she even taunt me like this? I should have known all along it's wrong to love her openly. If I would have kept it to myself this wouldn't have hurt so badly.

Day after day they spent time talking but usually in the open and usually where I had to see them. I tried to ignore what's going on, but it's eating my gut from the inside out. At first a week went by and then another. Next thing I knew it's been a month since I spent any time with her. We weren't even running anymore; I ran but not with her. Her maturity level showed, but if she really loved me she would quit playing these games.

She did come to help me work with Jack and Diane but every time it's all business. She did what I did without speaking to me. Not a disagreement even when I did something wrong on purpose. She just followed along without a word. Seeing her hair trace against her face, the way she wiped it away and looked back at me with those eyes. The distant in them kills me.

When I couldn't take no more I quit going up to the house for meals. I waited for Jarod to come in for bed which continued to be early evening. I would glare at him and he would avoid me. Obviously she has not told him or he wouldn't be spending any time with her.

Horse Play

49 Needed

Kyle had come down to the barn looking for me, "Kam, I need you to come with me. I am picking up a new horse today."

This came as a surprise. He didn't mention anything to me about a new horse. "You're getting another horse?"

"Yes, Sam picked him out."

Wondering what the plan is for purchasing a new horse I nodded went to the truck and got in without questioning him. If Samantha wants it and she gets it. He got in and glanced at me, cracked a smile, and then started the engine. He sat there for a moment. Hesitant he asked, "You're not going to contest this?"

Why would I contest it? Its job security for me and if I open my mouth I may say the wrong thing so I shook my head without a word. The ride was peaceful as I stared out the side window. With the hum of the tires on the road Kyle finally asked, "Do you have something wrong with your mouth?"

What is he talking about now? I turned to him not understanding. He gestured to my mouth and when I looked down at my hand it had blood on it. I licked my lip and shook my head. I really didn't want to talk to him about Sam and what we had gotten in an argument about.

"So, do you want to ask anything about this horse?"

I shook my head, "Sam gets what she wants."

"That is not true."

I rolled my eyes looking back out the window.

"Kamron, what is going on with the two of you, because Sam loves you and I hear her crying every night. Well, almost every night. It seems to be getting better, but that is not my point."

I shrugged my shoulders again.

"She said you insulted her?"

Now, that pissed me off, "No! Well, she may have taken it that way, but I was insulting the way she perceived something not her."

He raised his eyebrows, "I need more information than that if I am going to try to help the two of you out. She is not happy and neither are you, and what the hell is going on with Jarod here?"

Not wanting to explain the argument Samantha and I were having I went right into explaining about Jarod, "I didn't expect him to be here this long. He got in a fight with his step dad. I will call my sister tonight to ask when he can go home."

"That's not what I meant either. You are family and if he needs to stay with you I understand, but it isn't helping yours and Sam's relationship."

Cynically I huff a laugh. He was right because that is what started the argument.

"Are you going to fill me in on what is going on?"

I shook my head, "It's nothing that can be fixed. In fact I checked into getting an apartment in town."

He didn't ask me anymore questions. My chances of that getting back to Samantha are good. It's my way of telling her I will not live this way. If we were really over than I need to move. I couldn't stand to watch her move on with her life and still have feelings for her the way I do. Which reminds me of her, how blue her eyes are, how she melts into me when we kiss, how soft her lips are, the way her hair reminded me of summer flower, and how stubborn she is. How my favorite thing is to wrap my arms around her and listen to her ramble on about our future together.

Kyle laughed out loud as we pulled into the driveway. When I turned to him it became obvious that we both knew where my head is at. In fact this is probably a plan to fix Sam and my relationship and I just fell into it.

The horse's name is Buckaroo, and I quickly found out why. He is jumpy, fidgety, and guarded. I tried to sooth him but glared over the horse at Kyle, "Sam, wants this one?"

He nodded laughing.

"Why? It's obvious he is not trained at all."

"That's the idea."

Am I really this stupid? Sam wants to spend time with me and this is her way of demanding it. I laughed to myself and traced my hand down Buckaroo's face calming him, "You are my new best friend."

As unruly this horse is I wanted him as bad as Sam does and the horse got the vibe. He came around quickly with me and nudged my stomach. I grinned, "Something tells me you will be special to me and Sam." I pulled out a couple baby carrots patted his face and lead him out the gate and to the trailer. He stopped dead in his tracks and reared up. Getting him settle again took a few soft-spoken words, a strong hand, and a gentle touch. Kyle happen to be very happy with himself of this new adventure and laughed, "So how long would it take you to ride him home rather than spending the time here trying to get him in the trailer?"

He stood still while I saddled him up, but when I got on he went crazy. He bucked, twisted, and trashed his head back. Holding on for dear life I directed him towards the road.

The previous owner came running, "You might want to work with him before you ride him. He doesn't like to be ridden."

"Yeah, I got that. Kyle, I will see you at home." I kicked at his sides and he took off with the intentions that if he went fast enough maybe I would blow off his back. He ran hard and long. It's 20 miles from the ranch and he finally slowed. A calming walk took over the frantic race. Kyle pulled up alongside of us rolling down the window, "If you can do that already Sam is going to be disappointed."

Shaking my head in disagreement, "He got tired. I am sure he will still need a lot of work."

"Yeah, let's hope so or she will pick another one and I don't need any more horses."

I laughed and leaned down to glance in the cab of the truck, "Kyle thanks."

He smiled, "See you at home."

When Buckaroo and I got to the long driveway of the ranch Sam came running to me and my heart pounded so hard it felt like it wanted to leave me and stay with Samantha. Is this what we need to get along? To be working together all the time? She is smiling and bubbly making me drool a little. I miss her kisses so bad. I got off and lifted her to him taking the rains and leading them up to the barn with her on his back. She didn't say a word and I'm afraid that I might say the wrong thing again so I'll keep my mouth shut. The truth of the matter is I'm glad she wanted this horse. It means that there is still hope for us. Buckaroo is going to be our ice breaker.

We got him to the grooming room, and she helped me get him unsaddled, washed up, and brushed while we stayed silent. Avoiding my instinct to let my eyes take her in I only stole glances. She is so in her element with these large animals my heart filed with joy.

I startled when she spoke, "He is calm."

"Yes. I had to full out run him for most of the way home or he would have bucked until he threw me."

She grinned with that, and continued, "So he is high spirited?"

She's talking to me and I am giddy. Chuckling I commented, "You could say that. He will need a lot of work before you ride him again."

"Fine."

"Okay."

She walked around him and stood in front of me. My blood pupped in my veins so hard I could hear the pulse in my ears. Please Sam just say something to me? Yell at me if you need to, but please talk to me. Our eyes locked, and I fell deep in the depths of them drowning in the blue sea. Everything lost when she turned and walked away without a glance back at me. My heart ripped open inside my chest and took my breath away. This wasn't what I expected at all.

50 Flashback

I worked with Buckaroo every day to build trust with him. Sam came down to observe. Sometimes she adventured out into the ring working with him a little. He will be her horse so I had to let her, but my instincts stayed on high alert every time she entered the ring with him. Jarod came down to see her work with him but kept his distance never coming into the ring. When they sit together on the fence they spoke to each other, but Samantha's eyes stayed glued on me and Buckaroo. Every time I got a glimpse of Jarod's frustration my heart beat a little stronger making the grin on my face grow.

It has been a month of working with him. Today I have the saddle on him while we worked. He's not happy about it in fact he's not responding to my commands either.

Samantha yelled out, "Remember, you're supposed to guide him not direct him."

She will not use my line on me so I didn't look at her. Buckaroo shifting and pulling to the right I witness Samantha jumps off the fence heading towards me. Pulling him off to the side he reared up. If he will not behave she shouldn't be out here, "Samantha, stay back."

She glared at me with a snicker and continued to walk towards Buckaroo. His eyes went wide noticing her in his space. He turned to test where I stood and then back at her. He's looking for a way out. My muscles tensed while in my head I planned my rescue. Samantha walked right up to him and held her hand out to him. Odd as it maybe he lowered his head so she could stroke his nose. Her lips moved like she was talking to him so I inched closer. A knot grew in my stomach as I wondered what she is up to. She turned and with a firm voice she scolded, "Stay calm and relaxed because he senses everything."

She leaned her face against his neck, patted him gently, and then walked back to the fence. Gasping for air I realized I held my breath while she stood so close to him. I hate that we don't talk anymore; it makes her unpredictable and dangerous.

Jarod must have seen the interaction because he made his way to meet her at the fence. They both sat on top talking before Jarod ran off again. How odd that is. He must not have his chores done yet. That's good for me because I get Samantha to myself for a short while. I remembered back to when she was about 14 years old and we had just gotten Daisy.

"Kam, why are you doing that?"

"Because it helps to get them comfortable."

"So why lead her? You should ride her."

"No, you build trust then you ride."

I wanted to laugh at her because she was always full of questions. I traced my hand down Daisy's belly.

"Why do you do that?"

"Because it shows her I care about her and will be careful. Again trust."

I moved to her legs stroking them up and down one by one and checking her hoofs.

"Kam, she trusts you can we move on?"

"No. Trust takes time. Come here see if you can do it."

She moved closer, and I took her hand in mine and we ran it over Daisy's leg. "See, I don't work with her and she trusts me. So tell me again why you take your time with each horse because some don't need as much time as others?"

"You are right, but how would I know unless I give them time."

"Kam, do you have a girlfriend?"

That was the first time she asked me that personal question. She caught me off guard with it and I remember responding snapping at her.

"NO!"

"Why don't you have a girlfriend?"

I rolled my eyes, "When would I have time to have a girlfriend? I am here 24/7."

"Yeah, I guess, but you are a good-looking guy. I think you should have a girlfriend. You are old enough."

"Well, thank you, I think."

"Come on, Kam. Have you ever had a real girlfriend?"

"Yes."

"Tell me about her."

I shook my head. It isn't a pleasant memory. One of which she was seeing my best friend on the side. That's why I had to move away from there. This job came at the perfect time for me.

"Come on Kam. Was she pretty?"

"Yes, but I don't want to think or talk about her."

"Why?"

"Because, obviously it didn't work out and I don't want to dwell on the past."

"That's a good plan. Are you over her then?"

I laughed with a chuckle, "Yes."

"Well than its time to think of a new girlfriend."

I grabbed Sam around the waist from behind her and picked her up twirling her from behind, "Why should I have a girlfriend when I can get a million questions from you?"

She laughed and screamed until I let her down. She slugged me in the arm and then headed to the house.

At the time I did not understand her drilling me was her way of checking if I had feelings for her. Back then I loved her but not in the sense of wanting her to be my girlfriend. It was me wanting to protect her from jerks like my best friend. I glanced over at her again and she had an empty stare, but if my instincts are right she is up to something. Something told me to expect the unexpected because the storm is brewing and its name is Samantha.

Jarod came out of the barn yelling, "KAM! I need your help."

Torn between taking Buckaroo with me or worry and leave him tied to the fence. I glanced over to Samantha as my gut twisted more. Something is not right with her, "Samantha, promise me you will leave him here. Do not work with him until I get back. You got it?"

She didn't say a word. Is she still punishing me for my comment? Shit! "Sam! Promise me you'll wait."

She tilted her head, grinned with force, and glared. Not agreeing with me at all, but she got what I meant.

Then she forced the word, "Sure." She sounded plain as day like she didn't care to agree at all. I glanced over at her and she avoided my eyes.

"Sam, I mean it."

"Fine."

"FINE!" I forcefully blurted out, but headed to the barn.

As I walked with Jarod back to the barn he commented on how Sam is different this time. He complained that she wouldn't kiss him while showing me the clog in the hose. The more he complained about the distance she kept the better I felt. Her kisses sweet as strawberries, her eyes deep as the ocean, and her soft skin as silky as satin ran through my mind. As Jarod went through the steps he'd taken to fix the issue a sick feeling washed over me.

Not understanding where this sensation of nausea came from I rose to a standing position with my eyes on Jarod.

"What, Kam? What is it?"

I back out of the stable when it hit me. Samantha! Running to the pen to stop her from doing what she had planned all along. I'm so gullible; I should have known she'd do something like this. Hitting the gate it only took me two steps up to get over as I saw her mounting Buckaroo. A flashback of her accident rushed through my brain as I scrambled to get to her and Buckaroo. Samantha tried to get him under control, but he backed up and twisted, and turned and reared up.

She yelled at me, "I am fine. Let me ride him."

Grabbing the rains I pulled him back down working my hardest to stay calm so he wouldn't sense the tension between Sam and me. Reaching around the side of Buckaroo I grabbed for Sam's leg but she kicked free. Buckaroo came to my help if he understood or not and moved sideways until I gripped her leg more firmly pulling her off and into my arms as I let go of Buckaroo. His freedom welcomed as he trotted off, but I didn't let Samantha have her freedom. I held her tight, staring into her eyes.

She tried to yell at me but it came out soft and emotional, "Kam, I was doing fine. Shit, you are an ass hole."

She stunned me but I will not let her go. My own emotions raced from fear, to anger, all the way to hurt from her calling me an asshole. If I let her go now we may never settle this, and I am not letting her go ever again. Pulling her into me I wrapped every part of me around her whispering into her ear, "I don't care if you hate me Samantha. I love you."

Her warm hands came to my face cupping my cheeks in her warmth. She wrapped her legs around me when I lifted her as we stared into each other's eyes. Before I could react her mouth slammed into mine needy. She licked, nipped, and sucked until I couldn't resist her. My instinct took over, and I devoured her with my kisses pressing my lips against her mouth, her cheek, her eyes, and her nose. Everywhere I could plant a kiss on her I did.

That is until we heard Jarod, "Sam... Kamron... What's going on?"

Deflated, I closed my eyes and Samantha quit kissing me. I didn't want to face reality; I wanted her to keep kissing me. She unwrapped from me and slid down my body. Everything blew up in my face from not being able to stop myself from kissing her, or having her for myself. Letting her go right now is unbearable, but I let her go. When I could breathe again I turned to see her walk away from me.

Jarod yelled again, "What the hell, Kamron?" He took off after Sam asking her a bunch of questions. She didn't reply to him, she kept walking toward the back of the house.

Raking my hand through my hair I wondered *what the hell am I supposed to do now that Jarod witnessed that encounter of our entanglement.*

51 Apology

I didn't see her for a few weeks, and Jarod, well he is a little angry. He doesn't talk to me and he slams a lot of doors. He spends most of his time with Adam, which Tracy isn't happy about. She even chewed me out for not handling my problems myself.

Surprised by a knock on the door on a Sunday, I hope it's Samantha. We needed to talk about what happened or what will happen. My insides have been turning for weeks and I think I lost over 10 pounds from not being able to stomach food. The only things I do is work with Buckaroo and think about her. When I opened the door Samantha stood there. My heart leapt at the sight of her but she didn't even smile.

"Is Jarod here?"

"Sam?"

"Can you please go get Jarod?"

"Sam, please?"

She glared at me, "This isn't about you and me. I called his parents and they are in the barn office. Can you please get him?"

I left the door open and knocked on the bedroom door. Surprised when he walked out with his bags packed not even a glance at me as he walked pass me. Not sure what was happening I tried to follow them out of the shack. When I got to the door Sam put her hand on my chest, "You are not invited to this meeting."

"But it's my sister and nephew?"

She shook her head, "No, I handled this problem myself so you are not invited."

"Sam?"

"Kamron!" She pushed me inside the door and closed it. She took Jarod's hand in hers as they walked down to the barn. Did she decide to be with him after all? I would not stay here and not put up an argument. She is mine, she didn't love him, and I will not sit by and let this happen. I stormed out my door after they made their way into the barn. If I hurry I can catch what is going on so I jogged to the barn. When I approached the office Kyle's voice came loud and clear, but then Jarod spoke up next. Next my sister spoke enticing me to walk in the office. I'd like to see her too. Tyler's voice, the calmest of them all asked Jarod two questions, then Joslyn spoke again. All this talking but Samantha didn't say a word. Pressing my ear to the door I tried to hear anything from her. If she plans on marrying him I will storm in and put a stop to it.

Startled by Samantha hushed scolding from behind me, "Kamron?"

I turned to Sam wondering why she wasn't in the room with them. She shook her head and the only thing I could muster was, "Sam?"

She turned and walked away so I let myself into the office. Kyle mediated the conversation, but Jarod is going home. Relieved to find out he is going home alone and Samantha is staying here. It's the age that makes Jarod cocky enough to be stubborn, but he admits to over reacting and being stubborn. My sister's husband, Tyler, apologized for his short comings but missed Jarod terribly. Tyler is not Jarod's real father, but it's apparent that they care about each other and the one person they have in common, Joslyn. Tyler even offered to pay for college and confirmed he is always welcome at their home.

When everything had been decided I walked them to their truck I needed to say something to Jarod. I didn't know what to say, so I hugged him. When I let go he had tears in his eyes, "Do you want to know what she told me?"

I shrugged my shoulders. I didn't know if I could handle it.

"She said sometimes we do things for the wrong reasons and that if we are honest with ourselves that we would find the truth. She didn't love me, it's not what you think it was, and she used me for the wrong reasons."

My head pounded overwhelmed by this morning's activities. It's Samantha that took the responsibility of the situation earning my respect. She is growing up into an intelligent caring woman I hurt deeply. I needed to apologies to her about my judgment against what she thought was right at the time is wrong, but she learned something and handled it. He leaned into me, "She didn't say it, Kam, but I think she loves you."

I nodded and patted his back as he climbed into the truck. As they drove away my heart ached for hurting family, but he's young and will find someone to love as much as I love Samantha.

Pulled from my reserve by a firm hand on my shoulder, "It's hard to be away from family."

Nodding in agreement a smile touched my soul. Samantha is all mine again. She is my family.

"Do you think you two can work things out?"

Not wanting to show my weakness I glanced at Kyle while nodding. His eyes searched my face with understanding, "Well, good. I hope you'll take care of this today."

Not sure if that would I happened I tried to ease his thoughts, "I'll give it my best shot."

Nothing happened all day. All I did was work my day away. I thought with Jarod going home she'd come down and at least train with me, but not a peep.

That evening I fell down on my bed, a huge comfort after sleeping on the couch for the last seven weeks, however I couldn't sleep anyway. Tossing and turning with Samantha on my mind searching for the best words possible to apologize for my harsh words.

Up early I headed down to do chores when my eyes fell on her. Waiting with my eyes fixed on her she stretching for running, but it wasn't until her eyes met mine did I sense she needed her space. Her eyes empty of emotion all apologies slipping from my brain I headed to do my chores.

I took Buckaroo out in the late morning for some training hoping to see Samantha but she didn't show. How long is she going to keep this up? After lunch, which I avoided now Sam came wandering down. I got Buckaroo again and brought him out for more training. She stayed put on the fence observing but I wanted her to come down and make amends with him. If he will be her new horse she should gain his trust especially after that last stunt she pulled.

After the fourth day of the same ritual I had to change it. After she came down this time and I had worked with Buckaroo a little I walked over to her and handed her the reins. Confusion filled her face as her eyebrows furrowed, her eyes squinted, and her mouth pierced. I let myself out of the gate and walked to the barn. I wanted to look back, but I contained my urge until I was out of sight. She sat there for a long time talking with him.

I had to laugh to myself when she pulled a large red juicy looking apple from her pocket. She got down moving towards him. I stepped a little ways out from the door in case she needed protection. He is still temperamental. Buckaroo backed up, but she held the apple up for him to see. After that he battled his inner issues of wanting that apple and trusting her to get it. I could tell she was speaking to him as he bobbed his head up and down. Finally she gave it to him and he let her stroke his face. I walked a little closer to admire her connection with him. I moved closer and closer until I was leaning on the fence looking in between the railings.

"So, how is it going?"

With a jerk I hit my head on the fence noticing Samantha glancing over at me and giggled to herself. She took something else from her pocket but I turned to Kyle.

"I think better."

"Are you two talking yet?"

Shacking my head with no explanation and went back to watching her with him.

"Well, she doesn't say a word in the house either and it's getting weird so I wish you two would fix whatever is broken. I miss listening to her babble about her future."

"Was I part of that... before?"

He grinned and walked away. Great, what did that mean?

She made her way over, tied him to the gate, and opened it. I stood there waiting for anything she would give me. Hell, I would even take asshole again if she would talk.

"Thank you."

I smiled at her dumbfounded because I didn't know what to say. She moved closer and touched my cheek. I grew week in the knees and closed my eyes with the pain of missing her. Her hand moved away from my cheek but I wanted to keep her here.

"Sam, I am so sorry." When I opened my eyes she had already run towards the house. This left me even more miserable than before. She didn't stay long enough to hear my plea. I must try again soon.

52 Proposal

It seemed like this will not be fixed before she goes back to school unless I do something drastic. Every night I lay in my bed rehearsing my apology to her over and over again in my head. This needs to be perfect and I need to do this before she goes back to school, and the time is slipping away.

Just when I couldn't go another night of restless sleep a noise sounding like a knock came through my door. It couldn't be its late and it came too light. My head must be playing games with me because I want this so bad. There it is again. Could it be her? Leaping from my bed I stumbled to the door throwing it open. The thought of her excited me, but to find her standing there is unexplainable. Warmth filled me from my gut outward to every inch of my body. Wanting to grab her and pull her, but I stepped back allowing her to enter without me man handling her. Not ready for the outcome of this visit I turned keeping my eyes on her as she walked into the room, turning around to keep her eyes on me, and running her hand along my pictures. A memory of all the times she asked for a story.

When she reached the end of the shelves she demanded, "I want you to tell me one of your stories."
I couldn't deny her anything, "Which one? You know all of my stories."
She pulled a framed photo from behind her back, "I want you to tell me about this person in this collage."

When I took the framed photo from her my eyes grazed across tons of photos of myself, all of which recently taken. My eye met hers again, "When did you take these?"

If my eyes had been anywhere else I wouldn't have seen the slight twitch of a grin that appeared then disappeared in all of but 2 seconds. Taking her position on the love seat she waited for her story. As I sat down beside her I studied each picture trying to find what she wants me to see. Not in any of them did I appear to be happy. I was both sad and mad. I glanced up at her, "This is a very sad and lonely man that has lost something so precious to him it is hard for him to breathe."

Her eyebrows crunched together, "Tell me more."

"He is a man that doesn't think before he speaks and has a problem of admitting he was insensitive."

Her eyebrows softened, "So can he get better?"

"He wants to, but he isn't good at explaining what he meant to say."

I heard her huff to herself, "You got that right."

"What?" I wanted her to say it out loud, but she didn't.

She cracked a smile for another a second. "Can this person try to do it now?"

My throat went dry, and a lump kept me from sounding normal, "Yes."

"Well, he should get on with it."

"Right now?"

She raised her eyebrows, "Do you have a better time for him?"

"Okay, but I really suck at this."

She nodded and waited. I took a deep breath, "Sam, I am a jerk, or an asshole or whatever you think I am. I was insensitive because you were only doing what you thought was right. And you were doing it because you loved me and..."

She put her hand up to stop me, "That is an apology?"

I moved closer to her and took her hand in mine, "I am very sorry for insulting you in ways that were despicable. You deserve so much better than me but I can't even imagine you with someone else because it would kill me."

Her eyes squinted in a glare as she stared at me, "So you love me even though what I did you think is wrong?"

"Sam, it doesn't matter if it's wrong or right. I should have told you how I felt because it would never have happened if I had been truthful with you and myself."

She nodded and stood up pulling her hand from mine, "Then we start over?"

I nodded, but didn't have a clue what she meant.

"Jogging tomorrow than?"

That's starting over? We should spend time together now. She should stay and let me show her how sorry I am for hurting her. Show her I see her with new insight. She walked to the door, so I rushed to follow. I didn't want her to leave, not now or ever. She made her way through the door before I could stop her, but she turned reaching up on her tip toes to kiss my check.

Leaving me speechless, she headed to the house but glancing back over her shoulder she yelled, "You better be up by five. We start early around here."

She made me laugh. The first day I got here she said that same thing. We must start over from the beginning.

Samantha is going away to school in three weeks. That puts a strain on getting her to come around and asking her to marry me.

We run every day in the morning. She observed my training with Buckaroo for a few hours after running; she worked with him in the afternoon. In the evening we'd go for a ride down the lane. Sometimes we shared a horse and sometimes we didn't. As long as we have the time together I'd take anything.

We have one week before she heads to school, and I wanted her to know that I plan on spending the rest of my life with her. I planned a picnic packing dinner, a blanket, a bottle of wine, and the ring. Since our fight things have been different between us and Samantha has been more mature than I would have guessed her to ever be.

We road down the lane until we found our spot where I laid out the blanket, set up our dinner, and poured us both a glass of wine. Moving in behind her while she stared out over the flowing river I handed her the glass of wine and wrapped myself around her. We sat in silence for more than a half hour enjoying our time together and me enjoying her scent.

When her stomach growl I had to ask, "Sam, are you hungry?"

"No, I want to sit here a while."

She pulled my arms around her to hold her. I didn't want to push my luck with her but I traced my lips against her cheek and neck. The warmth of her grin grew beneath my lips. Needing to take this a step further, I scooted back and laid her down on the blanket I have urges way beyond my control and I kissed her, nibbling on her lips to make her kiss me more to which she did.

Curling up next to her to pay her the attention she deserved. I couldn't keep my hands off her as I traced my fingers along her face and neck moving down further. As I unbuttoned her top button I kissed her there. Her chest rose to my mouth as if her body wanted more. The softness of her skin tempting me to touch every inch of her so I unbuttoned another while placing butterfly kisses against her skin. An airy moan escaped her lips, her fingers tangled into my hair so when she gripped and pulled my head away from her she confused me. My eyes found hers full of disapproval. She has begged me to take her so many times and now she is angry with me for having a taste.

Lowering my mouth to her again she shook her head, "Kam, you will stop yourself, I will get frustrated and angry, and then you will feel bad for disappointing me gain. We need to stop before we get that far."

Affectionately I smiled at her, "Well, I guess we better eat."

When I sat up I pulled food out while she sat up buttoning her shirt. As I glanced back up, "You don't have to do that I like seeing your beautiful skin."

She shook her head getting up on her knees so she had better leverage as she shoved me back.

We sat, ate, drank, and enjoyed looking at each other. She is the most amazing person, my eyes scanning every inch of her body. From the way her shape is to how she holds herself full of confidence. When we finished dinner she curled up into my arms again and this time I fought the temptation to kiss her. I was happy to have her in my arms.

We had sat there so long while I tried to get up the nerve to ask her to marry me she fell asleep in my arms. Moving some stuff I laid her back down and wrapped the blanket around her. After packing everything up I moved back to Samantha I moved intending to carry her in my arms. She's so peaceful her face carried a slight smile while she slept. Wondering what she dreams about I swept her into my arms. Her response sweet and soft against my neck, "If I am sleeping how will I ride? Did you think about that?"

I laughed sitting her down on her feet. Hoisting her up I saddled up behind her. She relaxed into my chest as we road back to the house. My romantic proposal opportunity is over for the evening as I delivered her home.

Every day a step closer to departing day and every day my heart pounded a little harder. If I let her slip away without asking her it is my fault. The more I think about it the more I worry it's not the right time, or what if I say the wrong thing? No one gets down on one knee anymore, do they? Trying to come up with an amazing way to ask her to mine, and I keep coming up short and my time is running out. If I wait much longer she'll be at school and I'll be frustrated. I want her to know what she means to me before I ask.

Three days before she leaves, and she is spending more time shopping with her mom and packing than she has with me. I'm going crazy. No longer able to sleep I pace at night, no longer able to concentrate during the day, and when she is around I go silent.

Two days until she leaves and I am up tight. I jump any time someone says anything, and I don't hear a word. The only thing I can think about is asking Samantha to marry me. When she came down to retrieve me for dinner I jumped when my name left her lips, I jumped when she touched me, and I fidgeted as we walked to the house together. She could tell something wasn't right with me but she didn't push the issue. She trying to make the most of our time together and I'm being a fool.

53 Horse Play

Her last night and we have a storm coming. She helped me make sure all the horses were inside and safe for the storm. When she headed to the house I wanted to kick myself again for not asking her. They are leaving in the morning to bring her back to school and we had just parted for the evening. I sat on the front steps of my shack wondering what I could do before morning to impress her enough to say she would marry me. I forced myself to my room thinking about a plan. Kyle said he had a plan and her father helped him. I need to have a plan. We have talked about what we want so many times I could see it in my head. It will need to be a large barn with tons of stables, a clinic in one area, and an indoor riding rink on the other end. That's when I gave up and went to the kitchen area to draw up the plans. We'd have to have a house as well. Nothing gigantic like the one she lives in now, but one with three bedrooms for two kids and a nice living room.

Persistent knocking came from the front door in between the gusts of wind blowing outside. Grabbing all the papers I shoved them in a drawer heading for the door. Sam stood there soaking wet. I stepped towards her and pulled her inside wrapping a blanket around her.

She smiled at me, "My dad said you needed to talk to me before I head back to school."

Grinning, I rubbed her arms to warm her. She lowered the blanket showing the rain had soaked her to the bone. Her lingerie was clinging to her body showing every curve and translucent from the wetness. I tried not to notice, so I gazed into her eyes, "I don't know what to say?"

"Tell me the truth, Kam."

"What that I am in love with you?"

More determined she smiled, "That is a good start."

She took a step towards me and I backed up. I knew I had to keep my distance or I wouldn't stop. Not today and not with the way she looks. She continued to walk towards me but then she moved around me and glanced at me as she walked away from me toward my room. I closed my eyes trying to control the urges she inflicts upon me. I heard the rain hitting the roof harder and harder as the wind picked up and whistled through the windows. The clash and booms of the storm muffled the sound of my heart beat that pounded the blood through my veins. I turned to follow her into my room. She stopped beside my bed turning to look at me, "Kam?"

My lip twitched when I tried to smile at her but I stopped myself grabbing a towel to dry her off, and placed it on the bed temporarily. Letting my fingers trail her sides down to the hem of her lingerie top she lifted her arms while I pulled it up and over her head. Her body is perfect in every way. Her breasts where perfectly bulging slight underneath where her nipples where erect calling me to them. Almost stunned as my eyes trailed down to see the indent of her waist as it curved in a luring way for me to brush my body against. Turning her away from me I grabbed the towel, brought it to her hair and towel dried it as she tilted her head back. I kissed her forehead as I let the towel fall to the floor. My hands traced down her back following the curve with my fingertips but my mouth needed a taste. Planting kisses in the back of her neck and traced down her back as I lowered her bottoms to the floor. Only moving back up her body I could trace my hands against every curve of her body inching upward until my body spooned hers. Running my lips against her shoulder, up her neck to her ear, intending on driving her as wild as I feel, I brushed a soft kiss to her ear.

As she leaned into me she whispered, "Kamron, I love you."

With a shuttered breathed into her ear I replied, "And I love you."

Turning her to me I cupped her face in my hands as I kissed her soft moist lips. Her mouth opened for me and I gasped as I went in for a deeper kiss entangling our tongues into a dance of desire. Her hands and fingers glided down my sides bringing my blood to a boil as it rushed to my skin to meet her fingers.

I reached for the covers pulling them up for her to crawl in. She moved back making room for me to crawl in, but I pulled the covers over her while I stood there staring at her.

Her teeth moved over her bottom lip biting it, but then asked, "Kam?"

With a sigh of regret because she is so adorable lying in my bed naked with pleading eyes. I pulled back the top cover crawling in to lay with her. She turned to me a little, "Not even now, Kam?"

As I propped myself up on my elbow my fingers traced along her face admiring those beautiful blue eyes that invited me into the most pleasure of the deepest ocean.

She tried not to get irritated, but I could tell she's frustrated already. It came in her tone when she spoke, "Are you going to make love to me this time?"

Satisfied that I will show this beautiful woman how it felt to be made love to. When I leaned forward I grazed my lips against her face, "I am."

Taking her fingers in my I brought them to my mouth and kissed each tip like you would press a rip strawberry to your open mouth to cherish the juiciness of the flavor. Trailing my fingers along her arm, moving up and across her chest to see it rise in anticipation. Every part of her amazed me as I outlined her collar bone with my breath until I had filled her with warmth. I made love to this beautiful girl in ways she didn't know existed until her eyes no longer opened.

This will be my one and only chance to make her mine before she leaves in the morning. Whispering in her ear, "Samantha, will you marry me."

She shuttered with a sleepy reply, "Yes."

Huffing a chuckle I reached for the ring in my top drawer of the night stand, I took it out of the box, and slid it on her finger where I stayed and kissed for a while.

So relaxed in my bed she laid quietly wondering if she even understood what just happened I had to ask, "Samantha, do you want to see your ring?"

She moaned, "um... hun." But she never opened those eyes. She slept in my bed as innocently as an angle, my angle. My blue eyed, sweet tasting, sexy, stubborn, and yet determined girl.

I curled up to her wrapping myself around her. We didn't have sex, but I made love to her. I showed her that everything we shared that evening is me making love to her. The sex thing would come someday, but not today. Today I showed her what she meant to me without the horse play we'd get to soon enough.

Her whisper came as I closed my eyes, "Kam, I never slept with Jared."

The End

If you want to follow Melissa or get updates go to her web page @
www.mmmarlow.com

Melissa M Marlow:

Forever Yours
Wasting Away: Forever Yours book 2
Growing Tears: Forever Yours book 3
Push Away: Matters of the Heart
Losing You Prequel to It's Not Over
It's Not Over

www.ingramcontent.com/pod-product-compliance
Lightning Source LLC
Chambersburg PA
CBHW070603130626
46556CB00001B/257